HER LAST

WISH

(A Rachel Gift Mystery—Book One)

BLAKE PIERCE

Blake Pierce

Blake Pierce is the USA Today bestselling author of the RILEY PAGE mystery series, which includes seventeen books. Blake Pierce is also the author of the MACKENZIE WHITE mystery series, comprising fourteen books; of the AVERY BLACK mystery series, comprising six books; of the KERI LOCKE mystery series, comprising five books; of the MAKING OF RILEY PAIGE mystery series, comprising six books; of the KATE WISE mystery series, comprising seven books; of the CHLOE FINE psychological suspense mystery, comprising six books; of the JESSIE HUNT psychological suspense thriller series, comprising nineteen books; of the AU PAIR psychological suspense thriller series, comprising three books; of the ZOE PRIME mystery series, comprising six books; of the ADELE SHARP mystery series, comprising thirteen books; of the EUROPEAN VOYAGE cozy mystery series, comprising six books (and counting); of the new LAURA FROST FBI suspense thriller, comprising five books (and counting); of the new ELLA DARK FBI suspense thriller, comprising six books (and counting); of the A YEAR IN EUROPE cozy mystery series, comprising nine books (and counting); of the AVA GOLD mystery series, comprising three books (and counting); and of the RACHEL GIFT mystery series, comprising three books (and counting).

An avid reader and lifelong fan of the mystery and thriller genres, Blake loves to hear from you, so please feel free to visit www.blakepierceauthor.com to learn more and stay in touch.

BOOKS BY BLAKE PIERCE

RACHEL GIFT MYSTERY SERIES
HER LAST WISH (Book #1)
HER LAST CHANCE (Book #2)
HER LAST HOPE (Book #3)

AVA GOLD MYSTERY SERIES
CITY OF PREY (Book #1)
CITY OF FEAR (Book #2)
CITY OF BONES (Book #3)

A YEAR IN EUROPE
A MURDER IN PARIS (Book #1)
DEATH IN FLORENCE (Book #2)
VENGEANCE IN VIENNA (Book #3)
A FATALITY IN SPAIN (Book #4)
SCANDAL IN LONDON (Book #5)
AN IMPOSTOR IN DUBLIN (Book #6)
SEDUCTION IN BORDEAUX (Book #7)
JEALOUSY IN SWITZERLAND (Book #8)
A DEBACLE IN PRAGUE (Book #9)

ELLA DARK FBI SUSPENSE THRILLER
GIRL, ALONE (Book #1)
GIRL, TAKEN (Book #2)
GIRL, HUNTED (Book #3)
GIRL, SILENCED (Book #4)
GIRL, VANISHED (Book 5)
GIRL ERASED (Book #6)

LAURA FROST FBI SUSPENSE THRILLER
ALREADY GONE (Book #1)
ALREADY SEEN (Book #2)
ALREADY TRAPPED (Book #3)
ALREADY MISSING (Book #4)
ALREADY DEAD (Book #5)

KILLING (Book #6)

RILEY PAIGE MYSTERY SERIES
ONCE GONE (Book #1)
ONCE TAKEN (Book #2)
ONCE CRAVED (Book #3)
ONCE LURED (Book #4)
ONCE HUNTED (Book #5)
ONCE PINED (Book #6)
ONCE FORSAKEN (Book #7)
ONCE COLD (Book #8)
ONCE STALKED (Book #9)
ONCE LOST (Book #10)
ONCE BURIED (Book #11)
ONCE BOUND (Book #12)
ONCE TRAPPED (Book #13)
ONCE DORMANT (Book #14)
ONCE SHUNNED (Book #15)
ONCE MISSED (Book #16)
ONCE CHOSEN (Book #17)

MACKENZIE WHITE MYSTERY SERIES
BEFORE HE KILLS (Book #1)
BEFORE HE SEES (Book #2)
BEFORE HE COVETS (Book #3)
BEFORE HE TAKES (Book #4)
BEFORE HE NEEDS (Book #5)
BEFORE HE FEELS (Book #6)
BEFORE HE SINS (Book #7)
BEFORE HE HUNTS (Book #8)
BEFORE HE PREYS (Book #9)
BEFORE HE LONGS (Book #10)
BEFORE HE LAPSES (Book #11)
BEFORE HE ENVIES (Book #12)
BEFORE HE STALKS (Book #13)
BEFORE HE HARMS (Book #14)

AVERY BLACK MYSTERY SERIES
CAUSE TO KILL (Book #1)
CAUSE TO RUN (Book #2)

CAUSE TO HIDE (Book #3)
CAUSE TO FEAR (Book #4)
CAUSE TO SAVE (Book #5)
CAUSE TO DREAD (Book #6)

KERI LOCKE MYSTERY SERIES
A TRACE OF DEATH (Book #1)
A TRACE OF MURDER (Book #2)
A TRACE OF VICE (Book #3)
A TRACE OF CRIME (Book #4)
A TRACE OF HOPE (Book #5)

CHAPTER ONE

It was one of the rare days that Rachel was actually pleased with the woman she saw staring back at her in the mirror. She looked closer to twenty-five than her actual age of thirty-three and she was having a good hair day. She'd slept soundly last night and her brown eyes had a well-rested sparkle. Even her skin was on point today, glowing slightly under the bathroom lights.

Not that it mattered. She had training today and, in about three hours, she'd be sweating, and her hair would be in a ponytail. She enjoyed the training, though, and would gladly look like a sweating ragged mess if it meant she'd had a good session. She smiled at the anticipation of it, despite the awful singing voice coming from the shower behind her—the voice of her husband, Peter, belting out "Head Over Heels" by Tears for Fears.

"Darling," she said with a smile. "I love you dearly, but you missed that note by about a trillion octaves."

Peter responded by increasing his volume and reaching for a high note that wasn't even a part of the song. "You know," he said, following the note. "Most women would appreciate being serenaded before they go off to work."

"This is more like the torture techniques the army used in Afghanistan by pumping Marilyn Manson into prisons at three in the morning."

"Sweet. Let your supervisors know. Maybe I'd make a fine addition at the FBI. Then you could work around this singing voice all day long."

Before she could respond, Peter started singing again. When Rachel left the bathroom, there was a huge smile on her face. It was just one of those days…one of those days where even before the morning had gotten a good start, you just *knew* it was going to be a good day.

Despite the awful off-key chorus, she was actually glad to hear Peter singing in the shower. It was something he'd been doing a lot more as of late. They'd been working at having a second child for the past few weeks, which meant a much more active sex life. Their first, a daughter, Paige, had come after some difficulty, and they were hoping the second would be a bit easier. She knew Peter didn't mind putting in

1

the time trying to get her pregnant, but Rachel rather hoped it would happen soon.

When Rachel got downstairs, Paige was already awake. She was standing in front of the refrigerator, on her tip-toes as she tried to get the orange juice. She'd dressed herself, which Rachel always encouraged, and none of it matched. She was wearing a black *Descendants* shirt with a pair of striped leggings that were green and white in color. Her brown hair was still up in the pigtails Rachel had put in place the day before.

"Hey there, Squirt," Rachel said, stepping in behind her daughter and getting the orange juice down for her.

"G'morning, Mommy," Paige said.

"Glad to see you're already dressed for the day. You got big plans for the day?"

"No, just school," Paige said, though there was excitement in her voice. Paige seemed to love everything about kindergarten, which was good; she was just like her mother in that she did not particularly take instruction well. It was a trait that seemed to dissolve the moment Paige stepped into a classroom, though. Her teacher had nothing but remarkable things to say about Paige, something Rachel tried not to take too much pride in.

"What about this weekend?" Rachel asked, taking the glass of orange juice to the able where Paige was sitting with a bowl of Apple Jacks she'd apparently already poured for herself. Rachel cringed internally at the thought of drinking orange juice with Apple Jacks. "Anything big you'd like to do?"

"Mrs. Denning said I could come ride one of her horses, remember?"

"Yes, but I—"

"And Annie Jenkins is having an ice cream party. Oh, and I want to try that new jump park all the kids in my class are talking about!"

Rachel smiled. Her daughter always had huge plans. The girl hated to sit still—another trait she got directly from Rachel. "That *does* sound like a busy weekend."

Rachel set about made a smoothie while preparing a bowl of oatmeal. Because she had training this morning, she'd probably also eat a protein bar on the way to the obstacle course. She fully expected to be drained and maybe even flushed with adrenaline by the end of it, so protein was going to be key. She sat down at the table with Paige, enjoying the fact that she didn't need to rush this morning. Her training days started a little later than her typical day at the FBI field office, which gave her a moment to connect with Paige.

"We'll see about the horses," Rachel said. "I'll call Mrs. Denning this evening and try to schedule something."

"Thanks!"

Rachel ate her oatmeal as Peter came into the kitchen. He'd gotten dressed and was working on his tie when he came into the kitchen. He straightened the knot, and went about his fast and furious routine: a bagel slammed into the toaster and a tall cup of coffee. Rachel took a moment to watch him move quickly through the kitchen. He seemed to be in a good mood, too, which was great. He was so much more handsome when he was smiling (but then again, weren't all men?). He needed a haircut, but she didn't want to point it out. Besides, she liked it; his blonde hair hanging slightly over his forehead made him look boyish, younger than his thirty-six years. He needed a shave, too, but Rachel rather liked his five o' clock shadow.

Peter worked as a software designer, and as of late he and his team and been working on a patch for an update that, if finished on time, would net his business a massive multi-million-dollar contract with the US government. He'd been working late hours and acted as if he were caught in a whirlwind when he was home.

After lathering his bagel in cream cheese and topping off his coffee, he kissed Paige goodbye, giving her a little raspberry on her cheek. Paige giggled as he also put a dab of cream cheese on her nose.

He then quickly came over and gave Rachel a peck on the side of her mouth. "You ladies have a great day," Peter said.

"You, too, Daddy!" Paige said. "Hey, I might get to ride Mrs. Denning's horsies tomorrow!"

"That's fantastic," Peter said, already on his way out the door.

Paige frowned and looked down to the last remaining Apple Jacks, afloat in milk in her bowl. "Daddy was in a hurry, huh?" she said.

"Yeah. But we talked about that. He's been very busy with work. I think after another few weeks, it'll be back to normal. Now…speaking of hurrying, we need to get you to school. You want anything else to eat?"

"Maybe a donut from Dunkin' on the way?" she asked with a devilish smile.

"Only if we can be out the front door in less than two minutes," Rachel said.

Paige got up quickly and went screeching out of the kitchen and through the hall, looking for her shoes and bookbag. As usual, Paige was ready and waiting at the door before Rachel was completely ready. As Rachel finally fell in line and opened the door for Paige, her daughter beamed brightly and said, "I'm getting the Boston cream!"

Sneering at the remnants of her smoothie and the rectangular protein bar in her hands, Rachel did her best to share in Paige's enthusiasm.

***

Rachel thought it was a bit ridiculous that there was a car rider line for kindergarteners, but she supposed that's just the way the world worked now. As she meandered along in the line, Paige sat patiently for her turn to get out of the vehicle and walk into school. She had just finished wolfing down her Boston cream donut when she started pointing out her friends one by one (she had a lot of them, apparently) as they drew closer to the drop-off zone.

"That's Shelly! Her mommy has a cooking vlog."

"How do you even know what a vlog is?" Rachel asked.

Rather than give an answer, Paige continued to point out her friends. "Oh, and that's Micah! He's funny because sometimes he'll burp in class and never remembers to say 'Excuse me.'"

Just as they were about to fall into place for drop-off, a car in the exiting lane to the left stopped and gave a little beep of the horn. Rachel looked over and saw that it was Courtney Pinter, a way-too-involved school mom. She was rolling her window down and, not wanting to seem rude, Rachel did the same.

"Hey there," Courtney said in a tone befitting of a Disney princess. She was pretty and far too chipper. She was also only twenty-eight which Rachel also did not appreciate. "Just wanted to remind you that we need permission slips for the Summer Camp Crafts by next Tuesday! I know how sometimes those deadlines and dates get the best of you!"

The smile Rachel sent Courtney's way was about as fake as the too-chipper tone in Courtney's voice. *Ah,* she thought, *if only I lived a life where handing school paperwork was at the top of my priorities list. Must be nice…*

"Oh, I know," Rachel said. "We're going to be figuring out how to make that work over the weekend. Thanks!"

She rolled up her window and pulled ahead, one stop away from drop-off. "Mom, really?" Paige asked. "You're going to sign us up for Summer Camp Crafts?"

4

That Courtney is a real bitch, Rachel thought. She'd rather hoped Paige had forgotten all about Summer Camp Crafts—a three day camping trip for mothers and daughters.

"Well, like I told Ms. Courtney, we'll have to check our calendar and see, okay?"

Paige smiled so wide that her cheeks seemed to stretch. The smile was still on her face when Rachel pulled into the drop-off spot. Page opened her door with great enthusiasm, dragging her bookbag out with her.

"Bye, Squirt," Rachel said. "Love you lots!"

"Love you lots!" Paige echoed. She then took off running to catch up with one of her friends under the watchful eye of the drop-off watchdogs.

Rachel took three seconds to watch Paige enter the school. It was a sight that filled her with pride and sorrow in equal measure. She sighed as she pulled away and downed the last bit of her smoothie, wondering if she *could* maybe figure out a way to make Summer Camp Crafts work out.

***

Rachel walked out onto the training grounds and felt like a kid about to step out onto a playground. She'd run this course at least a dozen times before and had essentially obliterated it each time. She wondered if she'd be able to beat her personal best time today—a time that was the second fastest the Richmond, Virginia, branch of the bureau had ever recorded.

Earlier in her career, she'd come out and run the course for the fun of it. Nearly two miles of rugged woodland terrain right on the edge of Henrico County, complete with rope ladders, log obstacles, and a grueling quarter of a mile incline. At the end of it was a small open field where she'd then complete several firearms drills. Now, though, it was not for fun (though she did enjoy it). She'd been asked to run the course as part of a skills assessment required by the bureau.

The proctor was standing a few feet to her right as she waited at the start of the course. She'd spoken to him a few times before; his name was Griffith, a fifty year-old that had also once been an agent but had a debilitating knee injury that put him out of the game. He was typing something into a smart pad as he looked up to her. "G'morning, Mrs. Gift. You doing good?"

"Of course. Any day out at the obstacle course is a favorite."

5

"Glad to hear it," Griffith said. "As you know, there will be another proctor waiting for you on the other end. And this time around, there's going to be a bit more attention paid to your results."

"Why's that?" Rachel asked, already looking forward to the challenge.

"The higher ups know you have the second best time on this course. Because the first best is more than five years old, from an agent that's relocated to Salt Lake City, they've got their eyes on you. Between me and you, they'd be pleased if you broke *your* old record. But if you could beat *that* one…"

"Got it," Rachel said, already priming herself.

"Ready?" he asked.

Rachel gave a nod and readied herself into a runner's position. At the sound of the proctor's whistle, she took off without pause. Her muscles seemed to react joyfully right away. She'd read an article not too long ago about how experienced surfers often felt a surge of something very close to euphoria the moment they straddled their board and saw a wave starting to form nearby. She thought it might be very similar to how she felt whenever any physical task was presented to her.

She supposed it also helped that she knew the course well. The first portion was mostly flat woodland, a thin trail that wound through oaks and elms. As she came to the end of the first portion, her heart rate still pretty much normal and her breathing well-managed, she came to a drastic rise in the ground. Here, there was a rope that hung down along the ground, attached to a look-out station at the top of the hill. She made it halfway up the incline before grabbing the rope and using it to leverage her weight.

Next she came to a wooden wall that had been constructed right across the trail. There were two ropes or a series of handholds to choose from. Rachel opted for both, leaping up and planting her foot on the lowest handhold, and then grabbing the rope to propel herself upwards. She kicked upwards using another handhold and was over the top of the wall less than five seconds after touching it. The moment she came down on the other side, she was running again.

She took the following obstacles with the same precision and speed; she blew through the hurdles and scaled the rope wall as if she'd been doing it her whole life. She glanced quickly at her watch and saw that she was on course to beat her best time. But she was going to have to push even harder to beat the overall record.

When she came to the top of the incline, her calves were burning, but the sight of the open field up ahead numbed it. She saw the proctor all the way at the end of the field, standing in a protective barricade. All that sat between Rachel and the proctor were three wooden posts, all adorned with typical silhouette targets, and three half-walls to use as cover. She dashed to the first wall and drew her Glock from the holster at her hip.

Before she could bring it up and take position behind the first barricade, a stabbing pain flared in her head. It was so paralyzing and unexpected that Rachel's knees went out. As she fell to the ground, for a moment, all she saw was a blanket of white. The entire world went blank and then the sheet of white started to fade. It was replaced by what looked like shooting stars speeding right across her field of vision.

The next thing she was aware of was a man rushing towards her— the man she'd seen at the end of the course. "Agent Gift! Are you okay?"

He knelt down beside her, keeping his distance until he knew what had happened.

Rachel's vision slowly came back and she blinked away the last of those little white stars. A deep fear starting to rise up in her heart but she wasn't ready to process that yet. She couldn't even make sense of it.

"Agent Gift?"

"I'm fine," she said. "Pushed a little too hard…massive leg cramp."

She hoped it didn't sound too much like a lie. She was scared. No…she was terrified. The pain had been immense, like nothing she'd ever felt before, and the white specks and flash were somehow even worse.

She looked ahead and saw the three firing stations. She'd fallen less than twenty yards away from the end of the course.

But recalling that awful pain and the white spots and flashes, she had a sudden worry that it was the least of her problems.

CHAPTER TWO

Rachel was pretty sure that one of the more tense moments in a person's life was the handful of minutes following a CAT scan. It was bad enough that her primary care physician had seen her for ten minutes and then directed her to a specialist; that had placed a huge knot of worry in her heart. But now, sitting in a too-bright examination room while waiting for the neurological specialist to come back in, was like waiting in a cell to be led to the electric chair.

She felt fine, other than the nerves. Up until the point her doctor had recommended she see a specialist, Rachel was certain it would turn out to be nothing. Maybe just some random migraine that had blind-sided her and somehow affected her vision at worst.

But with each minute that passed, she became more and more certain there was more going on. Having to visit a specialist was scary enough. But waiting for them to come into the room for more than twenty minutes after a CAT scan was infinitely worse. A million different scenarios played themselves out in her head but they all felt ridiculous. The worst ailments she'd ever suffered were a fractured wrist and a very small surgery to remove a tooth when she was fourteen. She rarely even got sick, for God's sake.

The doctor finally came in exactly twenty-three minutes after the scan (Rachel knew this because she'd been checking almost obsessively). He had a folder in his hand and she was pretty sure she could see the white corners of her scan peeking out from around the edges. He was an older man, closing in on sixty, and had the sort of voice that was *made* for doctors—calm and reassuring with just an edge of authority. He'd introduced himself when she arrived but she had forgotten his name. Fortunately, it was right there, pinned to his breast pocket: Dr. Greene.

"Mrs. Gift, I have a few questions before we get to your results," Greene said.

"That can't be good, right?" she asked. Already, her heart was plummeting. It felt like it had been tossed into a mine shaft.

"The flickering lights you described...today was the first time you experienced them?"

"Yes."

"Any headaches as of late?"

Rachel thought about it for a moment and then shook her head. "None that stand out, no."

She could tell by the way Greene took the scan out of the folder that the news was not going to be good. As he revealed the scan, everything seemed to be moving in slow motion. "I ask," he said, "because I can't understand how something like this was missed."

Something like what?

She could have sworn she asked the sentence out loud, but apparently had not. For. minute, she could not breathe. She could not even quite fathom exactly what he was saying. How was any of this real?

He held the scan up to the light and took a pen out of his pocket. He used it to point at a portion of her brain. When he spoke again, he did it with the gravity of a man that had given similar news far too many times before. "Mrs. Gift, right here in the frontal lobe of your brain, is a rather sizable tumor. And I can't imagine how it has not caused you any ill effects until now."

She looked to the scan and even her untrained eye could see it. "Is…is that considered big?" It sounded like a dumb question now that it was out of her mouth, but it was all she could think to ask in that moment.

"It's among the largest I've seen," he said rather gravely.

"And is it…"

She couldn't finish the question. It was too hard to get it out, especially when she could already see the answer in his eyes.

"This type of tumor is referred to as a GBM," he said. "A Glioblastoma multiforme. They are very deadly and I'm afraid to say that yours is malignant." He spoke with the candor of a man that had delivered this same news far too many times. Oddly enough, Rachel pitied him for it.

"How…how long do I have?"

My God, am I really asking that question? she thought? *I was fine this morning. Hell, I was* great *this morning. How is this even happening?* She felt a tightening in her chest that she knew wanted to come out as wails and tears. She did her best to keep check on it as the conversation went on.

"There's no single answer to that question," he said. "It depends on if you want to try chemotherapy or other avenues."

"Is there any hope in those?" she asked.

He lowered the scan from the light and saw down in the lone chair in the room. "If we'd caught this about a year or so ago, there might be a chance. But as it stands now, I just can't say with any confidence that it would help."

The tiny bit of hope she'd clung to when she saw the scan in the folder died in that moment. She felt it happen. It was like heartbreak with a side of fear. Right away, she thought of Paige—of her daring daughter and the plans they'd made even as recently as this morning. Then, beyond that, another thought speared through her already-breaking heart.

Paige without a mother. My daughter is going to have to experience grief far too early in her life and...

No. She wouldn't think such things. Not yet.

"What about an operation?" Rachel asked. "Surgery?"

"GMBs are notoriously difficult to remove. There *are* surgeries, but with the size of this one, I can almost promise you that even if we could remove it, the surgery would kill you."

"Is there *any* hope?" she asked, her voice riding a wave somewhere between anger and sorrow. Her mind kept going back to how her death would affect Paige. Sure, there was Peter, too, but at least he'd experienced loss before when his mother died four years ago. But this...to leave a child motherless...

"Well, there are other specialists you can see," Dr. Greene said. "Doctors that specialize in trying to extend the lives of those with GMBs, for instance. There is, as I mentioned, chemo. And while the success rate with GMBs is incredibly low, I am never willing to one hundred percent rule anything out."

Rachel nodded, doing her best to stay sane and rational. "So how long?" she asked, trying not to break down and cry in front of him.

"The best you can hope for is a year and a half. It could be less, though. Maybe a year. I can give maybe a more accurate timeline with some more scans."

The tears came then, but she still managed not to start sobbing.

"I'm very sorry," Greene said, and she felt that he meant it. "Is there anyone you can call that can help you process this?"

She nodded, wiping the tears away. "My husband. He can...but...but, he..."

"I am not telling you what to do, Mrs. Gift. But I would call him. Have him come pick you up. You're welcome to use my office or one of our patient rooms to process through it and discuss next steps."

"No. I'll call him, I just…need a second. Can I have this room for a bit?"

"Of course. Please let me or my nurses know if there is anything we can do."

He gave her a final look that she supposed was meant to be some sort of sorrowful encouragement. When he closed the door behind her, the trauma of the news came slamming into her heart and mind. She let out a singular wail and then held the rest in as images of her daughter— bright, happy, smiling, full of dreams—filled her head. She rocked back and forth on the edge of the examination table. She only reached for her phone a single time, fully prepared to call Peter. She could still hear him singing in the shower, echoing in her head, and for some reason she did not want to tell him. She did not want to throw this grenade into their orderly lives.

No…not over the phone. If she called and told him he needed to come pick her up, he'd know something was wrong. For now, she'd get herself together and go home. She'd find some way to tell him at dinner—him and Paige, both.

And with that thought, the tears came faster as something within Rachel felt like it was breaking.

CHAPTER THREE

As she slid the dish with the prepared ingredients into the oven, Rachel thought she might start crying. She'd chosen something simple—baked spaghetti, one of Paige's favorites—and it was still a monumental task to focus on the ingredients and bake times. Making dinner with the weight of the doctor's devastating news was unbearably difficult

How was she supposed to tell Paige that she wouldn't have a mother in a year or so? How was she going to have the talk with Peter and start figuring out how to move money around, how their insurance would—

The front door opened as Peter arrived home from work. Rachel heard Paige squeal "Daddy!" at the top of her lungs and then a series of little footsteps as she ran to greet him. It was a sweet little bit of monotony, the same way every Monday through Thursday afternoon played out. Paige pretended to attack Peter, Peter dropped his bags and picked her up, spinning her in circles until he deposited her on the couch.

Rachel listened to it all as she set the oven timer. She the wiped the counters down and took out plates for the table, anticipating the last part of the weekday routine. It came, just as expected. Peter came into the kitchen, gave her a playful tap on her backside, and kissed her cheek.

"Good day?" he asked.

"Mmm hmm." Tears stung her eyes as she said this and she made a point to keep facing the cabinets as she took out the plates. "You?"

"Busy, but not too busy," he answered. "Mostly just meetings to figure out who we're going to get to write up these proposals. Which means the next few weeks will be absolute hell. And maybe a few after-hours sessions at the office. So just a heads up."

"Baked spaghetti for dinner," she said. "I know it's not your favorite, but I was in a hurry and it's Paige's fa—"

"Nonsense. Sounds delicious. I'm going to run up and get changed and I'll set the table."

She watched him rush out of the kitchen and up the stairs, likely wanting to make sure he got back downstairs to set the table before she did. Peter was a good husband and tried to make sure she never felt like all of the household items such as cooking, washing dishes, and laundry came down to her. He helped with a bit of funkiness in his attitude, but she'd almost stopped noticing it after a few years of marriage.

She left setting the table for him, standing just outside of the entry between the kitchen and living room. She watched Paige in the living room, perched on her knees in front of the coffee table. She was coloring while also watching a show about magical cheerleaders. Her tongue stuck out of her mouth just a bit, a trait that had apparently been passed down biologically from Rachel.

I can't do it, Rachel thought. *I can't tell her…*

It then occurred to her that she was going to have to do this twice. There was no way she could just drop the news on both of them at the same time. That could be a potential disaster, Peter having to process it while also trying to help Paige understand what it meant. She'd have to tell Peter first, just the two of them. Then after they'd processed it and got their share of grief and sorrow out of the way, they'd figure out the best way to tell Paige.

Peter came down the stairs moments later, oblivious to Rachel's dreamlike state. She shook it off as well as she could and managed to keep it together until they all sat down to dinner. Rachel did her best to go through dinner as if it were any other day. And while she had decided to tell just Peter first, she could not help but picture the scene. Sitting alone in the living room, or in the bedroom just before bed. *I found out today that I have a large tumor in my brain.*

She imagined Peter's reaction and something about it did not sit well with her. Just thinking of his face collapsing in grief, of his weeping and confusion, made her somehow certain that she would not be able to tell him. It wasn't fear, but a love for her husband—for her family. As an FBI agent, there had been two times during her career where she had been placed in a situation where she had to tell someone that a loved one had passed. It was one the hardest things she'd ever done and for reasons she could not quite identify, this was infinitely harder.

"…and the lady on the video said the Dole Whip was the best food in the park!"

Rachel was barely even aware that Paige had been speaking. She also saw that Paige was looking directly at her. *Dole Whip,* Rachel thought. *Park. She's taking about Disney again.*

"Yeah, but just ice cream?" Rachel asked, trying to sound as casual as she could.

"With *pineapple*," Peter said.

"Yeah! So can we please put that on my list?"

Paige had an ongoing list of things she wanted to try when they took her to Disney World for her eighth birthday. It was still two months away, but she had been planning for it as if it were tomorrow. She'd created playlists to listen to on the drive down and had recently started watching YouTube videos about how to enjoy your Disney trip to the fullest. The tongue-out-of-the-mouth concentration thing had come from Rachel, but the girl's knack for planning was a direct result of her father's DNA.

"Yes," Rachel said, fighting emotion. "It can go on the list."

She wasn't sure why, but something about Paige's planning struck a nerve in her. Her daughter had made plans that she, Rachel, might not even be around for. A wave of sorrow bigger than any other she'd experienced all day rose up within her and she knew she was not going to be able to keep it down.

"You okay?" Peter asked, looking directly at her.

"Yeah," she said, putting on a smile that felt far too fake. "Just zoning out. Just…"

She felt it rising up—not the words, but the heaviness of it all. Had she just decided not to tell Peter? Had she made the decision to not burden him with this? Or was it just that she was a coward?

"Rachel?" Peter said, concerned now.

"I'm not feeling the best," she said, the excuse coming quickly and without much effort. Getting out of her chair, she said, "I need to run to the bathroom."

She was pretty sure Peter called out to her again, but she didn't hear it clearly. She headed for the stairs, not liking the idea of retreating into the downstairs bathroom to have a complete breakdown. The tears were streaming before she made it to the master bathroom off the bedroom. A low moan had started to rise up in her throat, barely audible as she opened the bathroom door. When she closed it behind her, she sat on the floor with her back against the sink cabinets. She bit back the wailing that wanted so badly to come out and wondered how long it would take for Peter to come up. She thought about Paige and wondered what she might be thinking in that moment.

She rocked herself a bit, back and forth, picturing Paige with a pair of Mickey ears and walking through the park holding Peter's hand. She was not in the picture, nor was she in the imagined moments of Paige's high school graduation, first boy troubles, or practicing her slow-dancing with Peter in the living room before prom.

And as all of those images rolled through her head, Rachel started to understand why she was so afraid to tell her family about the tumor—about her very shortened lifespan. It wasn't only the breaking of their hearts and the disruption of her family. No, at the very core of it was the feeling that she was letting them down in some intangible way.

She wasn't sure how much time passed between closing the door and the soft rapping sound that came from the other side. It felt like only a few seconds but her shortness of breath and tear-streaked cheeks suggested otherwise.

Peter's voice followed the soft knocking on the door. "Rach, are you okay?"

"I think so," she said. She was ashamed at how easily the lie came out. "It's my stomach and head. Maybe a virus or something. I don't know."

"Sick to the stomach?"

"Maybe," she said. It made her feel guilty, but she wished he'd just leave her alone for a bit. If she could just cry it out and deal with it on her own, it would be easier. Maybe then she'd be able to bring herself to tell them.

"Let me know if you need anything," Peter said cautiously through the door.

"I will. Thanks. But if this doesn't let up, I think I'm just going to go to bed."

She heard Peter's footsteps walking away from the door. Rachel allowed herself a few more moments to lose herself on the floor. She stifled back her cries, wishing she was home by herself to just let them all out and get acquainted with the idea of death without her family there to make it hurt so much.

CHAPTER FOUR

Lucinda Masters quietly walked out onto her back deck with a pack of cigarettes in her hand, moving with stealth so as no to wake up her husband. Not that it mattered—if he hadn't stirred awake when she got out of bed at 1:15 in the morning, he wasn't going to hear the door to the deck open up one floor below. There was a chill to the late spring air, but not an unpleasant one. Still, it made her wish she'd grabbed her robe—coming out in a tank top and a pair of her husband's boxers wasn't exactly toasty.

Lucinda had not been sleeping well for a month or so, but it had been especially hard tonight. She'd finally made that damned appointment. She'd been hoping she could avoid it, figuring that the result of Kel's sperm test would come back with their answers. But when his results had come back totally fine, her worst fears had been realized; their inability to have children was all on her.

She fumbled with the pack of cigarettes and lit one up in the darkness. She hated the habit and only had a few a week. She figured if things went well tomorrow and the following days, she'd have to give the habit up. She was fine with that, though. It was a small price to pay if it meant she and Kel could get pregnant.

Taking a deep drag and puffing it out into the night, Lucinda wondered if thirty-nine was too old to be making a push for pregnancy. It made her regret waiting so long. Until two years ago, she and Kel had both agreed they never wanted to have kids. But something had changed in both of them and now here she was, Lucinda Masters, age thirty-nine, with an appointment with a specialist the following day.

As she took another drag, she realized that though she was tired, she did have a good feeling about tomorrow. She and Kel had made their change of heart on kids unprompted and at roughly the same time. It almost seemed destined to work out. She wondered if—

She heard something to the right, just beyond the deck. She walked in that direction, wondering if the damned racoons had come back. They'd been a menace to the neighborhood last fall, tearing through everyone's trash cans. She walked to the railing, nudging past the grill, and looked over.

At first, her eyes did not understand what she was seeing. She'd been expecting to see a racoon or two—so when she saw the figure of a man standing right there at the edge of her deck, there seemed to be a hiccup between her eyes and her brain. And by the time she figured out exactly what she was seeing, the man was reaching up towards her.

Lucinda let out a cry of surprise, the cigarette falling from her mouth, but it was cut short by the sudden pain along her scalp. It felt like she was being skinned alive up there and it took the sudden jerking motion and then her falling over the side of the deck railing to understand that the man was pulling her by her hair. When she fell, the scream tried to come out again. But when her back and head struck the yard six feet below, all of the wind went rushing out of her.

She stared up to the night sky, the stars twinkling dully, trying to gather her breath. As she tried to get up, the man fell on top of her. He drove a knee into her stomach, and the pain in her lungs, begging for air, was like nothing she'd ever experienced.

But then she felt something slip into her stomach. It was sharp and somehow cold and she felt it slicing through her muscles. There was a tight pinching sensation as something vital was pierced. Somehow, it hurt even worse when the man drew the knife out. He leaned down closer, his nose almost touching hers. His breath was in her face but all she was truly aware of was the knife going in again…and again.

Lucinda thought it might have gone in a fourth time, but she wasn't too sure. By that time, the stars overhead were growing dimmer and the sky seemed to fall slowly down over her and swallow her up.

CHAPTER FIVE

The bedside clock read 4:15. She wasn't sure when she woke up, but the little sleep she got had been fragmented, broken. Rachel turned to her right and looked at Peter's sleeping shape. The sheets covered him from the navel down and she took a moment to appreciate his body. He had never been one to worry about abs or muscles but he'd always been blessed with an unreal metabolism and managed to seem to be in at least decent shape. She toyed with the idea of reaching out and stirring him awake but couldn't do it. She was tired and stressed— the perfect recipe for caving in and telling him the terrible news.

Coward.

It was a word she called herself many times during the course of the night. Oddly, though, Rachel was okay with it. Untimely death had caused enough damage to her family long before she'd been married. Her mother had died in a boating accident just two days after Rachel's eleventh birthday. Her father had done his best to run things as a single father but had abandoned her, leaving her with grandparents that, though they loved her fiercely, had not been prepared to raise a child while in their sixties. While her mother's death had been unexpected, Rachel thought it might be even worse to *know* it was coming. To tell your family you were going to die in a year—that set up a morbid little chain of dominos that knocked over plans and future visions, hopes, and dreams.

She thought of the trip she and Peter were supposed to make to Montego Bay for their twelve year anniversary next year. She thought of Paige's Disney trip, of summer camp activities…and in the pre-dawn hours of morning, they felt like little bees stinging her mind. Somehow, she managed to finally drift off to sleep. She fell into a dream instantly and it was like falling into a pool of icy water. She was sitting on the deck of the boat that her mother had died on. Her mother was also there, sitting across from her with a bottle of wine. She drank directly from the bottle as Rachel looked at her.

"It's about time you met me out on the boat," her mother said. Her blonde hair was in a ponytail and she looked absolutely radiant—just as Rachel remembered her.

"But…you know what's going to happen here, right?" Rachel asked.

"Of course I do. It happens to us all. And between you and me, I'd rather go out with my mind and body intact than in a hospital bed when I'm ninety, everything falling apart."

"But aren't you scared?"

Her mother laughed and took a long gulp of wine. "No. I'm sad more than anything. Sad that I won't get to see you grow up, sad that I never got to touch your father again. But you…you still have time left."

"The tumor…it took my time away. My time is *its* time. I'm just an oven to keep it cooking."

"You were always a little overdramatic. Rachel…you have a year. Use it. Use it *wisely.*"

"What about Peter and Paige? Do I tell them?"

Her mother smiled and when she did, her form started to fade away and the boat began to fall apart. "What am I?" she said. "Your mother?"

Her laughter faded away with her. In its place, as the boat started to deteriorate, some sort of alarm started to sound from the boat. For a fleeting instant, Rachel hovered above the water, the boat fading like her mother into the nothingness of the dream.

She searched for the alarm but when she realized what the noise was, the dream fell away.

Rachel sat up in bed, reaching to the bedside table for her phone. She only had two numbers unblocked on her cell—Peter, and her supervisor at the bureau, Director Anderson. Because it was clearly Director Anderson and, according to the bedside clock, was 5:50 in the morning, she assumed there was something big on the other end of the line.

Do you even care, though? she asked herself.

On the heels of that, she heard her mother from the dream.

"You have a year. Use it wisely."

As Peter started to stir at the sound of her phone, she answered it quickly. "This is Agent Gift."

"Gift," Anderson's voice said, not sounding sleepy at all. "I know it's early, but I need you and Rivers to get to Baltimore as early as you can. We've got a double homicide that needs wrapping and the local PD is at a loss. I told them I'd get someone up there to assist as soon as I could. You and Rivers need to swing by the office first for a quick briefing."

The defeatist part of her that was refusing to look beyond the tumor told her there was no point. Was she really going to go on assignment and pretend things hadn't changed?

Yes, she thought, looking back over to Peter. *Yes, that's exactly what I'm going to do.*

"Yes, sir. Does Rivers know yet?"

"I'm about to call him now. And case reports will be emailed to you within half an hour. Thanks, Gift."

She ended the call and got out of bed. With the promise of a new case within reach, she didn't feel as tired as she knew she should. As she walked over to the closet, she heard Peter shift in bed.

"Punching the clock early?" he said groggily.

"Yes. I need to get to Baltimore as soon as I can. Are you okay to call the sitter for this afternoon?"

"Yeah, I can do that."

"Sorry it's so early," she said.

"It's okay."

She took her clothes out of the dresser and walked over to his side of the bed. She kissed him softly on the corner of the mouth and he smiled. He then rolled back over on his side, seeking out another hour of sleep before he had to get up. Rachel walked into the bathroom and closed the door behind her. She dressed quickly, feeling oddly at peace with the decision she'd made—a decision that she had rally not wrestled with all that much.

Her background in psychology told her that she was being selfish. She knew that if someone in her situation came to her for advice, she' tell them to do the exact opposite of what she was doing. What she needed to figure out for herself in order to handle keeping such a secret was if she was telling no one was out of a form of denial or just a way to totally avoid the issue.

Whatever the reason may be, so long as she was able to function at a normal capacity, the tumor was going to be her little secret. It was a secret she'd keep from her family as well as the people she worked with. Yet as she dressed, she thought of her mother on the boat, both fading away in the dream.

"You have a year," her mother had said.

Looking in the mirror as she slipped into a button down shirt, Rachel looked into the mirror with a thin frown and said, "Use it wisely."

***

20

When Rachel stepped inside the Richmond field office and made her way back to the conference rooms, she felt like someone was walking on her heels. There was no one there, of course; it was merely the secret she was keeping. Having not told Peter, the tumor now seemed as if it were an actual person, shadowing her wherever she went. She did her best to shake it as she hurried into Conference Room A. Someone had already started a pot of coffee and she was not at all surprised to see Jack Rivers standing by it, filling a cup.

She and Jack had been partners for a little over a year now and had met the same bureau milestones at roughly the same time. They'd barely known one another during the academy and training but when they had been partnered together out of the Richmond branch, it had seemed like a natural fit. Jack was the sort of thirty-three year old that you could just tell was a geeky guy in high school and college, just now starting to understand that he was a rather good-looking man that people were starting to respect. It did not mean, however, that he had dropped the comic banter that Rachel had come to rely on to keep her in a good mood on even the toughest of days. The slight pudge in his cheeks suggested he'd once bene overweight—something he always poked fun at himself about. He referred to himself as a former fat kid that had left the weight behind, but not the sarcasm-as-a-defense-mechanism or his love for obscure music and sci-fi movies.

He looked to her as she came to the coffee pot and grimaced. "You look like shit, Gift. You just wake up?"

Rachel showed him her middle finger just as Chief Director Anderson came in. He was looking over a printed out report as he walked to the front of the room. He was very good at his job and treated all agents under him with kindness and respect, but he was not the sort of man to waste a single second of time. Even before he had sat down and taken his eyes away from the report, he was talking. Rachel and Jack sat down right away, Rachel not yet having time to doctor up her coffee. She sipped from the bureau brew totally black, and thought it might be the equivalent of sipping jet fuel.

"We've got two dead women in Baltimore—one aged forty-one, the other aged thirty-nine," Anderson said. He finally looked away from the print-out and to his two agents. His brown eyes were full of energy and, as always, a little intimidating. "Both were stabbed multiple times in the stomach. The bureau is being called in because of the timespan between the murders. Based on the bare bones details that exist, it's believed they were killed within twenty to twenty-four hours of one another. Obviously, there are worries that it could be a serial, but the larger boiling point is the small window of time that passed between them."

"When was the latest victim discovered?" Rachel asked.

"Around three thirty this morning. It's all there in the report. Because this one is two and a half hours away, I don't need you coming back to the office. Stay in Baltimore until it's resolved. If either of you have issues with that, let me know now and I'll have you replaced."

"Good to go," Jack said.

Rachel thought about it for a moment. It would be nothing new for her to be away from home for several days. Because of her job, Peter and Paige were both used to it. Over the last three years or so, her work as an agent had caused her to stay away from home for periods of more than three days about a dozen times or so. But with her current medical news and the war that was raging in her head over whether or not to even tell her family—

"Gift?" Anderson was looking at her curiously. "You good?"

She figured taking a case that would remove her from home for a few days might actually work out in her favor. Time away from Peter and Paige as she tried to figure out what to do might be the very thing she needed. And God, she hated how absolutely selfish that made her seem.

"Yes, sir," she said. And then, covering her tracks a bit, she added: "I'll just need to make some calls on the way to make sure my husband and I can secure childcare while I'm away."

"Sounds good," Anderson said. "All of the details and case reports have been emailed or texted to you...so don't let me waste your time. Get going."

They did just that, leaving Anderson alone in the conference room. Jack headed out first, with Rachel trailing behind with her still-black coffee. And even heading down the hallway with Jack in front of her, she could not shake the feeling that yesterday's prognosis was falling in behind her like a stubborn shadow.

CHAPTER SIX

Jack Rivers hated driving, but Rachel had always enjoyed it. It was yet another way their partnership was a good fit. Something about being behind the wheel and watching the roads and highways unfold in front of her was calming to Rachel. It also helped her concentrate on the case details as Jack read them, going through each and every file Anderson had sent them. Getting out of Richmond wasn't as hard as it could have been, as they missed the morning traffic by about half an hour. The Beltway, she knew, was going to be a completely different story.

"These photos are pretty gruesome," Jack said, wincing at the current one on his screen. "A lot of blood. Forensics reports eleven stab wounds, all in the stomach."

"Which victim?"

"The most recent, from last night."

"What about the first victim?" Rachel asked.

"Nine times, same place. Right in the stomach."

Rachel tried to form a link to it all in her head. The women being slightly older helped her to categorize it a bit easier. Typically, women murdered at such an age were targets of some sort of terrible domestic abuse rather than intense and unrequited lust. But two of them so close together, and killed in similar ways, presented a whole new side of the puzzle.

"It's also worth noting," Rivers said, "that both women were killed at home. The first victim was laying in the kitchen, the second in her back yard. It looked like she may have fallen from the back porch…before or after she was killed, though, is anyone's guess. She was also killed late at night, apparently when going out for a cigarette."

Rachel did her best to stay focused on the details Jack was giving her but every ounce of mental strength she had seemed to still be digesting yesterday's news. She was also hyper-focused on the road, as if her brain was betting on the monotonous actions and scenery to help process the information faster.

"Rachel?"

"Yeah?" she asked, quickly glancing at him. His brown eyes were studying her in a way she rarely saw. It was far too close to the way he studied victims and suspects—with a suspicious glint in his stare.

"What's up?" he asked. "You seem pretty distracted."

Crap, she thought. *That didn't take long.*

"No, I'm okay. Just tired, I guess. I didn't sleep well last night."

"Up all night trying to make a baby with Peter?" Jack asked with a knowing chuckle.

She grimaced and shook her head. She'd almost forgotten she'd shared that bit of information with Jack. But sometimes, all the time alone in cars managed to open up a lot of personal information. She trusted Jack with her details, though. He was a very honorable guy once you got past the oddly-timed jokes and Marvel movie references.

"No. Just not a great night for sleep, I guess."

He scowled at her and said, "I don't buy it."

"I didn't ask you to," she said, trying to inject humor she simply did not feel.

As she turned her eyes back to the road, she could sense his eyes lingering on her for a moment. She found it sort of touching that he could so easily tell that something was bothering her, but she also wished he'd drop it.

And that's exactly what he did. He finally turned his eyes back to the digital files in front of him and only spoke when he came across something interesting. Just like that, she'd lied to her partner, too. She figured that was why she could feel the presence of the tumor in the car just as she'd felt it back at the field office. Now it sat in the back seat, leering at her, just as big a part of her work life as her home life.

Maybe I should tell Jack first, she thought. *We have to trust each other with our lives, so any sort of secrecy could hurt our chemistry. It would also be a decent test-run to figure out how to tell Peter and Paige.*

There was some sensibility to the thought but she still fought it hard.

"Victims were living in different parts of the city," Jack said, breaking the thought apart. "It appears one was divorced and had recently re-married. Initial reports—and they are *very* initial, as the ones for the second victim are barely four hours old—indicate no links or similarities in their lives or social circles."

"The divorce is certainly worth looking into," she said. "I think it might be—"

The ringing of her cellphone interrupted her. Figuring it had to be either Peter or someone back at the field office, she didn't even bother looking at the call display before answering. "This is Agent Gift."

"Rachel Gift?" a male voice asked.

"Yes. And who is this?"

"It's Dr. Greene. I'm very sorry for calling so early but I wanted to touch base with you before my day got away from me."

Rachel felt like she was being caught in a lie. She felt her cheeks going red at the sound of Dr. Greene's voice and instantly wondered if Jack could hear the doctor's voice. She glanced in his direction quickly, but he was still looking through some of the files on his iPad.

"Well, it *is* rather early," she said, hoping to quickly end the conversation without wanting to seem rude. "What can I do for you?"

"I wanted to touch base to see if you had any other questions after having the night to think it all through."

"None right now, no."

Her answers were coming quickly and with very little pause between his questions. There was a slight pause from his end and then a very brief sigh. "Okay. Well, if that changes, feel free to call my office and I'll be happy to set something up. I'd love to have you come in so we can talk face-to-face about some of your options."

He'd barely gotten the s-sound out in *options* before Rachel responded. "I'll be sure to do that. But at the risk of sounding rude, I really do need to go."

"Of course. Enjoy your day, Mrs. Gift."

She ended the call and placed her phone in the cupholder in the center console.

"I take it that wasn't Anderson or anyone at the office?"

"Nope. Family stuff. Which reminds me...I need to call Peter and fill him in to sort out a babysitter and school stuff for Paige."

Jack nodded. He was accustomed to being present for brief family-oriented calls. He even made a habit to speak with Paige every now and then if a call to her daughter during work could not be helped. She picked her phone back up and called Peter and when the phone started ringing, she could all but actually *see* that other presence in the back seat, the personification of her tumor, taunting her and asking how long she really thought she could keep up the lies.

CHAPTER SEVEN

Because the scene was obviously fresher, they visited the home of the second victim first. When they arrived, local PD was scattered around the back yard. The body had been moved, but the area where the victim had fallen was marked off with tape. There were also splatters of blood on the bright green grass that appeared almost startling under the morning sun.

A sickened-looking officer gave them a suspicious glance as they stepped towards the area, coming around the side of the house. Rachel showed her badge and the look dropped away; he let them into the back yard. The three other officers looked to them, an elder-looking one stepping in their direction right away.

"You with the FBI?" he asked.

"We are," Jack said. "I'm agent Rivers, and this is Agent Gift."

"I'm Sergeant Owen," the elder-type said. "Glad you made it so quickly. We're starting to worry this is going to get out of hand."

Rachel looked back down to the ground and saw one particularly large streak of blood. The grass around the area was slightly compressed. It made her think the victim had not died right away; she'd been alive for at least a few minutes, dragging herself across the yard, likely towards the stairs.

"How long ago was the body removed?" Rachel asked as she took in the scene. The tape to mark the body was no more than two feet away from the edge of the deck. She supposed the drop was somewhere around ten feet.

"A little after six this morning," the officer said.

"And where is the husband?"

"He's got a sister that lives in town. She came and took him away about the same time the body was removed. He was understandably a mess."

"Any chance you think he's a suspect?" Jack asked.

"I never rule out a husband. He was a *new* husband, you know. The victim, thirty-nine-year-old Lucinda Masters, got divorced from her first husband not too long ago. She and her new husband, Kel, had only been married for four months."

"Any other family been by?" Rachel asked.

"Lucinda's sister was blowing up Kel's phone earlier. She was pretty broken up, too. But no one has come by."

"Thanks," Rachel said. "I think we'll just have a look around for now."

"Help yourself," Owen said, waving a gesturing hand at the house. "Our initial scan of the place showed no signs of break in, no signs of a struggle—nothing. We asked the husband if he could see where anything had been taken, but he was clearly not in any condition to give an accurate answer."

Rachel and Jack walked up the back deck stairs. The lighter Lucinda Masters had apparently used to light her cigarette was still on the deck rail. It was a passing thought, but Rachel wondered if she had come outside because they simply didn't smoke in the house, or if she was doing it in secret—hiding it from her husband.

They stepped into the house and found exactly what Owen had insinuated. The place was very clean, the only clutter coming in the form of a few dirty dishes sitting in the sink, waiting for their place in the dishwasher. Rachel checked both living room windows, then the doors; there was no sign of forced entry. They then made their way into the bedrooms and bathrooms. There was nothing to be found there, either. Yet, as Rachel looked through the bathroom and opened up the drawers along the bottom of the double sinks, she found a bottle of One A Day prenatal vitamins.

"The victim was thirty-nine, right?" Rachel asked.

"Right," Jack answered from outside the bathroom. "Why?"

She showed him the bottle of vitamins. "I don't know if there are many women close to forty that regularly take prenatal vitamins."

"Yeah, but it's not *impossible,* right?"

"No, I guess not," she said, putting the vitamins back. "You know, we can look inside all we want, but we're not going to find anything. He attacked her outside. He just walked around house and waited. That's the feeling I'm getting anyway."

"Waited or got there at just the right time," Jack said. "Can't rule out that he *knew* she'd be there, smoking."

"Smoking *and* taking prenatal vitamins," Rachel said. "That's not an equation that really adds up, now is it?"

Jack shrugged and walked further down the hall. Rachel stayed in the bathroom a moment longer, trying to figure it out. She supposed the vitamins could be old—that she had not taken any of them in a while. Then again, if she'd just remarried and moved into a new home with another man, the vitamins seemed like something that would have been

27

thrown away when she moved. The bottle had been about half empty, so she supposed trying for a kid might have been on the agenda with her new husband.

Rachel retraced her steps back through the house and walked back out onto the back porch. She saw Sergeant Owen in the yard, speaking to another officer that was typing something into his phone.

"Sergeant Owen, did the husband mention anything about doctor's appointments?"

Owen looked up to her and shook his head sadly. "Honestly, he didn't say much of anything. He went from absolute shock and sadness to a bitter sort of anger."

It made sense. Rachel had seen the exact same thing in the reactions of men that had lost their wives to murder. The initial heartbreak opened a door to anger—an anger that was really, at its core, the sharpest kind of grief imaginable. If Owen's description was correct, it made Rachel already feel that the husband wasn't a suspect, though they'd certainly have to talk to him at some point.

Jack stepped up behind her, looking down into the yard. "Initial thoughts?"

"None yet," Rachel said. "But I do feel that the murders being so similar and occurring so close together have to be linked somehow."

"Want to go see what the coroner has to say?"

"Yes, and then maybe Lucinda's husband. If he's as wrecked over this as Owen says he is, we'll be wasting our time going to him right now."

As they passed back through the back yard and gave their thanks to the police, Rachel handed Sergeant Owen a business card. "When the husband is ready to talk, please give him my number."

Sergeant Owen nodded, pocketing the card. As Rachel walked away from the scene, she realized that the time they'd spent at the Masters' residence was the longest stretch of time she'd spent since yesterday's doctor's visit not intensely focused on the diagnosis. The case was already proving to be the distraction she needed. Deep down, she knew it was not healthy (neither physically or mentally) to avoid it in such a way. But for right now, she felt normal; she didn't even feel that leering presence she'd felt in the car on the way to Baltimore, her personified version of the tumor always following her.

What she inherently understood but refused to face as she and Jack got back into the car was that at the end of this case—no matter how it turned out—she would have a grim truth to face. And there was no amount of work or exciting cases that was going to change that.

28

CHAPTER EIGHT

The body of Lucinda Masters lay on the examination table, telling a brutal story. Rachel had long ago learned the lesson that the extremity of violence was rarely captured in pictures, no matter how expensive the camera or how gruesome the scene. Seeing the body with your own eyes was so much worse; it removed the filter of distance and replaced it with intimacy. It was no longer a body on a screen or a print, it was *right there* in front of you, a very real and bloody thing.

The coroner stood to the back of the room as Rachel and Jack observed the body. Lucinda had apparently kept in good shape; she had toned legs and arms that looked vaguely muscular. Her breasts, though obviously affected slightly by age, showed no signs that she had borne children or nursed them. Again, Rachel thought of the prenatal vitamins in Lucinda's bathroom.

"As you can see," the coroner said, "the cause of death is quite simple. Multiple stab wounds. Even without an official autopsy, I can look at the angle and bleed rate to determine the internal areas that were affected. Clearly, the lower abdomen was targeted, though not with any sort of precision. The stomach has been lacerated, both kidneys punctured, intestines cut in several places, and I'd suspect the uterus has also been badly damaged."

"You said there was no real precision," Jack said. "What makes you say that?"

Even before the coroner answered, Rachel thought she knew. Killers that knew what they were doing typically stabbed in certain areas, and they did it in a way that each stab would pierce something vital. What Rachel saw on the table in front of her was the work of a man with no clear path of attack. He'd just stabbed blindly.

It reminded her of something from her past—one of the cases that had so far defined her career. It was a case she always thought of time and time again. Whenever she allowed her mind to go there, it was accentuated with the face of a frail-looking man staring at her through thick glasses, a smile on his face that chilled her.

"The wounds are made by an amateur," the coroner said, breaking apart Rachel's thoughts and stopping her from revisiting that dark place. "Blind rage. I'd also suggest that the knife he used was rather dull. There are a few wounds that almost look as if she was impaled by something rather than stabbed with a knife."

"Is the first victim still accessible?" Rachel asked.

"Yes, come this way, please."

The coroner led them out of the primary examination area and led them down the hallway, to a larger room. Inside, what looked like several small metal doors were installed into the wall. Rachel had been in more than her share of these and knew this was body storage area. If she'd had any doubt, the drastic change in temperature would have clued her in.

The coroner walked to one of the drawers, pulled the latch, and the drawer popped open a bit. When he slid the drawer open, a long slab came rolling out smoothly. The first victim, Gloria Larsen according to the report, lay before them, her skin slightly blued from the chill of the storage compartment.

"Same thing here," the coroner said. "Hastily stabbed all about the abdomen. I do believe it took her longer to die. The lower cut just below the stomach would have been painful, but would not have bled as much."

Rachel counted the stab marks and nodded. "And she was stabbed less than the second victim." She turned to Jack and said, "Which means the killer grew more confident with the second body."

What she thought after this, but did not speak out loud, was that the confidence he displayed on the second body meant there was a very good chance there was going to be a third. And probably a fourth and fifth and beyond if they weren't able to catch him.

Again, she briefly thought of the man looking at her through thick glasses—a man named Alex Lynch. A man that had haunted her dreams three months after the case had been closed. A man that had done the sort of unspeakable things she'd only read about in case studies during her time in Quantico.

She closed her eyes against the thought of notorious mass murderer Alex Lynch and shook the thought away.

"The report I have says she likely dragged herself across the kitchen floor," Jack said. "There was blood smeared on the tile. We saw the same thing at the Masters' house—a smear of blood across the grass from where she had presumably tried crawling to the stairs. Do you think there's any chance the killer is doing it on purpose? Stabbing them in a way he *knows* isn't killing them right away?"

"I doubt it," the coroner answered. "Again, the sloppy way in which the stabbing was conducted makes me think he was just letting himself

30

go wild. I don't believe the areas in which these women were stabbed was pre-mediated."

Rachel understood what he meant and actually thought he was right. She did find it peculiar, though, that the stabbing had been contained to the stomach. Why not the chest? Why not the back? Why not slitting their throats?

As Rachel considered all of this, her phone buzzed in her pocket. It was not a number she recognized, but began with a Baltimore area code.

"This is Agent Gift," she answered.

"Hey there. It's Sergeant Owen. Sorry to bother you, but Lucinda Masters' sister has gone from blowing up the husband's phone to now calling the station. They patched her through to me and she's being very insistent. I thought it might help with the case if you spoke to her. What do you think?"

Rachel thought a grieving sister looking for some sort of vengeance was not the best lead, but she also knew that they didn't have much to go on and this was a killer that was going to be very active.

"Tell her we'll be by to talk to her in about an hour. You got an address?"

***

Jessi Parker lived in a nice two-story home, three miles away from her sister. When Rachel and Jack arrived, she was waiting for them in her living room. She was drinking a strong-smelling tea and regarded them with red, puffy eyes when Rachel and Jack sat down on the couch across from her. From elsewhere in the house, Rachel could hear the murmured voices of a man and child—presumably Jessi's daughter and husband.

"We understand that you were relentlessly calling Kel in the wake of your sister's murder," Rachel said. "And then the police. While I understand you're going through quite a lot, I have to ask if there is any reason for it. Do you have any leads or information that can help us find who is responsible for this?"

"No, and you see, that's just thing." Jessi Parker was frantic and highly emotional. Her words were coming out quickly, all slurred together. She was an emotional mess, and Rachel was going to be very surprised if they gathered anything of note from speaking with her. "Lucinda didn't have enemies. I know it's the sort of thing a grieving sister is supposed to say, but I mean it. Lucinda was the sort of woman

31

everyone loved. And to think that someone jut decided that she didn't need to live anymore…"

Jessi stopped here and slammed her hands down on the coffee table. The strike was hard enough to cause her cup of tea to jump slightly, some of it sloshing out.

"Mrs. Parker, did the police tell you that Lucinda was not the first?"

She nodded, wiping fresh tears away. "Yes. And that somehow makes it worse."

"A few days ago, there was another woman murdered in the exact same way. Her name was Gloria Larsen. Do you happen to know if your sister knew a woman by that name?"

Jessi's red eyes squinted hard in concentration for a few moments but then she shook her head. "I don't recognize that name. Kel might, but…" She shrugged, as if she really didn't expect much from Kel, either.

"We also understand that Lucinda's divorce from her first husband had been finalized last year and the marriage to Kel is only about four or five months in. Do you happen to know what cause the first marriage to fail?"

"Absolutely. When Lucinda and George—her first husband—were dating, they agreed on everything about their future: where they'd live, how many kids, pets, and all of that. But something changed after marriage and George changed his mind about having kids. He decided he did not want any, but Lucinda stood firm. They fought over it for the better part of twelve years until it sort of became a poison to their marriage. She left him and when she did, I think she originally planned to go the sperm bank route and have a child and raise it on her own. But then she met Kel, and everything worked out. From what Lucinda had been telling me, she and Kel started trying for a kid almost right away."

That explains the prenatal vitamins, then, Rachel thought.

"Any idea where the first husband is these days?" Jack asked.

"He moved to New York almost immediately after they separated. And my mind went there, too. Did George do it? But no…despite their constant arguing, George loved Lucinda very much…even at the end, I think."

"You don't think jealousy of another husband might have driven him to it?"

Jessi gave another of her non-committed shrugs and said, "I suppose anything is possible, but I'd find it very hard to believe."

"And what about Kel?" Rachel asked.

"I don't know him well enough to judge. But I do know that Lucinda fell for him very fast. She seemed happy—which was great because she'd been so miserable once she turned thirty-nine. She felt that she'd wasted so many years and that her biological clock was nearing its end. She finally found some happiness and then…"

She shook her head and Rachel could tell she was struggling with more emotion.

"It's okay," Rachel said. "You've actually helped quite a bit and we'll leave you to your grief now."

Grief, she thought. *If you told your family about the tumor, this is the sort of thing you'd be causing them.*

She felt selfish by even making the comparison, so she got up and headed for the door. "Please, Mrs. Parker, let us know if you think of anything else."

"I will," she said, but she was already starting to weep.

Rachel, not wanting to leave her there alone, waited until her husband poked his head out of the kitchen down the hallway before leaving. Jack followed and they headed to their car, ushered out by Jessi's wails.

CHAPTER NINE

As Rachel drove away from the Parker home, Jack looked through the case notes and located the phone number of the first victim's husband. Rachel listened to Jack's end of the short conversation. She was always amazed at how he was able to shift gears, to put the light-hearted and often goofy personality behind to turn on kindness and compassion when appropriate. It was almost like working with a robot sometimes.

When the call was over, Jack said, "The husband of Gloria Larsen is Doug. He's currently staying at his mother's house. Speaking to him for that little bit made me think he's of a mostly rational mind and he says he's good to speak to us—maybe even eager."

"Good. I think we may need to check in with Kel Masters after this, though. We can speak to everyone listed in those files, but he's going to be the best bet."

"Local PD insinuated that he didn't have much to offer in regards to the case," Jack pointed out.

"Maybe after a few hours of being able to process it all, that will change."

Jack left it at that and they continued the short drive to visit with Doug Larsen in moderate silence. In between residences and with no active conversation taking place, Rachel started to again feel the pressure of her diagnosis. She wasn't sure what it was that she felt more pressed to tell Jack than her own family, but it was beginning to make her feel uncomfortable.

They reached the home of Doug Larsen's mother less than fifteen minutes later. Somehow, it had already come to be noon and Rachel felt that the day was quickly getting away from her. Even she could sense some of her own urgency when she knocked on the front door. It was answered by an older woman with a worried look on her face. Her eyes seemed to say *"Oh, it's you"* as she opened the door wider for them.

"You're the FBI folks?" she asked.

"Yes ma'am," Rachel said. "Is Doug still here?"

She confirmed that he was and led them into her home. It was a nice house, and well-cared for. Pictures of family were hanging everywhere and the smell of something baking was radiating from the kitchen. Banana bread, if Rachel's nose was correct.

They found Doug Larsen sitting at his mother's kitchen table. His hands were wrapped around a mug of tea as he looked out over a flowerbed in the back yard. He looked to be in his early-to-mid forties and he, like his mother, looked worried and very tired.

"Make yourselves at home," the mother said. "Can I get you coffee or tea?"

Rachel and Jack declined as they sat down at the table. Doug finally turned his weary eyes in their direction and offered the closest he could get to a smile.

"Thanks for meeting with us," Jack said. "We'll do our very best to keep this as short as possible."

"I'm in no hurry," Doug said glumly. "It's not like I'm going anywhere."

"Have you been back to your house ever since it all happened?" Rachel asked.

"No," Doug said. "I'm sure you know that I was the one that found her. There was just so much blood and...and I can't even think about going back there."

"The police records indicate that you didn't find anything stolen...that nothing seemed out of place. Is that correct?"

"As far as I could tell. Not to seem like an ass, but I wasn't exactly taking inventory of our stuff. I found her on the kitchen floor, bleeding more than I thought possible. When I saw her like that, I went to her and saw that she was already dead... my brain sort went into lockdown, you know?"

Rachel nodded. For now, she assumed they'd be okay to trust the police report. If the case truly stalled on them, they could go to the Larsen residence later and have a look around.

"Can you think of anyone that might have had a grudge against your wife?" Rachel asked.

Doug shook his head and said, "You know, the cops already asked me all of this. And I'll tell you what I told them: I can't think of a single person that would have done this."

"Had you noticed any changes in her demeanor over the last week or so?" Jack asked. "Did anything seem sort of off?"

"Not that I could tell. You know...I keep going through the contacts on her phone, trying to imagine any of these people that would have either done this or might have known. No one pops up, though. And even if I thought someone *might* know something, what the hell am I supposed to do? Call them and ask, '*Hey, you didn't happen to have anything to do with the murder of my wife, did you?*'"

"You have her phone?" Rachel asked.

"Yes. It was the one thing of hers I managed to take with me when the cops helped me get out of there."

"Would you mind if I had a look?"

"Whatever you need," Doug said. He fished around in his pocket and took out his wife's phone. It was an iPhone with daisies printed on the case. A pop socket clung to the back with the infamous yellow smiley-face on it. He tapped in his wife's passcode and handed it over to Rachel.

She went to the collected texts and scrolled through them as Jack continued asking questions. She listened along as she scrolled for any answers. Jack asked if there had been any strange activity in their neighborhood, if they had a security system, if his wife had ever told him she felt scared or threatened. As Doug answered *no* to all of these questions, Rachel could find nothing of interest in the text threads that had been saved to the phone.

Yet, when she went to the call history, she found something of note. Scrolling down, she saw that all of the recent incoming and outgoing calls were from people that had been saved into her contacts list. The one exception to this was the very last number Gloria Larsen had called before she died. It was a local number—the area code was proof of that—but it was not a saved contact. Based on reports, Gloria had been killed somewhere between five and six in the afternoon. This call had been made at 4:17.

"Mr. Larsen, do you happen to recognize this number?" Rachel asked, showing it to him.

He leaned in and studied it closely, but shook his head. "No. I have no idea."

"You mind if I call it?"

Doug thought about it for a moment. She figured he was trying to determine if it might be the number to someone he wasn't prepared to hear about. Maybe a secret lover? Maybe something worse?

"Yeah," he said, the word barely coming out at all. "Go ahead."

Rachel called the number and elected not to place it on speaker mode. She remained in her seat at the table and listened to the phone ring on the other end. It was answered on the third ring by a woman's voice.

"Regency Fertility Clinic, how can I help you?"

36

The link snapped in Rachel's head like a puzzle being put together. Just like Lucinda Masters, it appeared that Gloria Larsen had been trying to get pregnant. She thought about introducing herself, giving her badge number, and asking for whatever information they had on Gloria Larsen—appointments, check-ups, anything of that sort. But she figured they should ask Doug about it before going that route.

"I'm so sorry," Rachel told the woman. "I have the wrong number." She hung up and looked to Doug, handing the phone back to him. "That was Regency Fertility Clinic."

Brief knowing came across Doug's eyes and he then blinked away tears. He took a deep, shaky breath and looked to the phone. "Yeah. We'd been trying to get pregnant. For a few years, actually. The doctor said it wasn't a hopeless endeavor...but that we'd have to work at it because the chances were pretty low. We'd talked about fertility treatments but...well, I didn't know she'd been speaking with them."

Rachel chose her next words carefully, aware that she was treading on sacred ground. "I understand something like this is very personal. Would you like to call them back and ask how long Gloria had been contacting them, or would you prefer for us to do it?"

"You," he said right away. He was again fighting tears back. "I don't know if I could deal with the weight of that. I mean, I just finished a few calls for the funeral and..."

"Of course," Rachel said, getting to her feet. "We'll head over there, just to see if there's anything that can help with the case."

"Do you think there could be?"

Rachel didn't think it wise to let him know that the other victim had also been dealing with pregnancy issues, so she kept it simple. "When we don't have answers, we just have to exhaust all possible options. So we'll just have to wait and see."

"Thanks for your time," Jack said.

They turned to see the mother standing there behind them. Rachel assumed she'd been there the entire time, listening. Without a word, she led them back to the front door. She was pleasant enough, but it was clear she wanted them gone so that her son could sit alone with his thoughts.

Getting back into the car, Jack said: "Two women, both trying to get pregnant. I'd say that's a pretty solid link."

"Same," Rachel said. "But why? And how did the killer know?"

She slid behind the wheel as they shared a look. It was not a look of excitement, but one they had shared any times before—one that communicated motivation and urgency. It was a look that said: *"Let's go find out."*

CHAPTER TEN

The individual that had killed two women in the span of three days worked nine hours every weekday in an Advanced Learning school. Once, in a time that seemed like a lifetime ago, she had worked as a teacher in an elementary school, third and fourth graders, with an experimental year as an art teacher that had gone bust. She'd always had a passion for kids, even now.

Murder was new. It had only been a part of her life for about a week and a half now. It had been much easier than she'd been expecting. It wasn't fun, per se, but it was something that exercised the mind. She'd had to truly do some soul searching over the last several days and while murder was not an enjoyable act, it was far from the brutal evil act so many movies and television shows had made it out to be.

Currently, she was teaching a class of fifteen highly gifted students how to code. The kids were an average age of seven years old, the sort of children that truly did show promise but would likely have that promise crushed when they made it to middle school and all they cared about was impressing the opposite sex—or, in the case of one of the little boys in the class, the *same* sex. It was already quite clear.

Working with children while harboring this deep, dark secret provided an odd sort of thrill. There was shame, sure. She knew what the higher-ups might think if the secret was ever discovered. How could you teach kids so well but also so easily take life? Honestly, it was something she still considered herself when she was unable to sleep. There was no real answer—or at least not one that could be learned and processed in the course of nine days.

Besides, she would never hurt these children. She cared deeply for these children and every single child that had come through this classroom in the past five years. The children had been nurtured with the love and care their parents likely withheld from them by working too hard or not taking the time to speak to them.

But while she loved the children, they were also like a cancer—a cancer that ate at her from the inside out. She'd learned nearly a decade ago that she could not have children. Even if there was a suitable lover (which there had not been for a few years now), there was no hope for children in her future. It was the only reason teaching had made sense; it was a way to be around kids, to enjoy their smiles and stories and their wide-spanning dreams of a future they naïvely believed was going to be bright and shining.

After coding, there would be some nonsense that the school liked to refer to as Independent Thinking. What it was, essentially, was time to goof off...which was perfectly fine. Half the fun of being a child was goofing off a bit. At this age, they should not be consumed with excelling at miserable tests the state used to measure their intellect. It seemed especially stupid for these children, who had already proven they were leaps and bounds above the other kids in their grade.

She loved the kids, but hated the school system. It was just a place for kids to be stored while their mothers and fathers were out milling away to pay outrageous bills and mortgages so they could fit in and catch up with those slightly above their social class. These children would all grow up with the scars of that system on them, affecting the way they viewed politics and justice, love and sex, respect and hatred. She saw this every single day and it was why she had initially convinced herself that she did not even want to have children. They were born into this world destined to already be screwed up in a million ways. So if she could not have any of her own, maybe it was for the best.

But these kids were different. These were the sort of kids she would have surely enjoyed raising. Special. Independent. Not just carbon copies of their messed up parents. The thought of it was both inspiring and depressing all at once.

She sat behind the small oak desk and watched the kids at work. Sometimes, one would look up, as if for recognition or encouragement. She would smile brightly even though her thoughts were elsewhere. Her thoughts were on plans for the night. There was already another woman out there, another that she would visit.

Thinking of how the night would play out, her smile widened even when there was no child looking back.

She found herself smiling often these days, as a way to cover up the horrific things she had done. But she had to. She'd made a mistake recently and she had to correct it. No one else would...that was for sure. That's when she'd started killing those women—when she realized she was the only one that had the power to correct her mistake.

She'd had a moment of weakness several months back and *that* had been the first true mistake.

Of course, her mother might tell her that the first mistake that started this whole mess was going out to the bar that night during her freshman year of college. She'd not been old enough to drink, of course, but a short skirt in a college town was an easy work around for such a problem. She'd only had three drinks, but it had been enough to cause her knees to wobble as she made her way through the back alley with her friends, a shortcut back to the dorms.

Her knees had still been wobbly, her head still a little off kilter, when the three men stepped out of the shadows. One served as the lookout while the other two raped her and her friend. And then they alternated. Her only mistake had been trying to fight back when they switched places. For that, she'd received a head slammed against a brick wall that resulted in fifteen stitches. She'd also received cuts and bruises between her legs, one cut receiving five stitches. And she'd also received the news that she would likely never be able to have children.

Maybe her mother would be right. Maybe the visit to the bar had been the very first mistake. The very bad decisions she'd made of late had stemmed from that bad news from the doctor. Her choice in men had been affected, as had some pivotal life decisions. But then there was the really big mistake—the thing she'd meant for good but had come back to burden her and cause her to kill. The—

The bell rang. She snapped out of her dark thoughts and for a moment she had no idea where she was.

School. The children...

The kids got up in an orderly fashion and put their laptops away. They then exited the class, chattering and laughing. A few waved to her and one young boy that seemed particularly drawn to her even gave her a fist bump.

She'd really wandered off there. It had never been that bad before. She wasn't sure how many more she was going to have to kill but she certainly hoped her work would be over soon. If not, she wasn't sure how long she'd be able to separate these two very different sides of her life. Even as she watched the children file out of the room, her mind was already wandering towards the plan of how to take the next life and what it might feel like to take just a single moment to truly enjoy that first push of the knife as it pushed through skin and muscle, tissue and life.

CHAPTER ELEVEN

There was a small group of protesters outside Regency Fertility Clinic when Rachel and Jack arrived. There was nothing destructive or overly boisterous taking place, just a gathered group of about a dozen people with Pro-Choice signs. Rachel wasn't quite sure why, but their presence aggravated her—not that she was vehemently on either side of that debate. It was just an unwanted and unexpected source of noise and distraction from the case.

That slight irritation followed her inside as she and Jack entered the clinic. The place was cool and air conditioned. The small waiting area outside of the appointments and reception area was decorated in a cute farmhouse style. Pregnancy and childcare magazines filled the small tables by the chairs.

As they approached the reception window with the smallest line— the window all the way to the right, only containing one other person— Rachel was bombarded with something else she did not expect. She felt an overwhelming depression trying to dig its claws in. Being here in the midst of hopeful women and couples that were fighting to do what they could to bring life into the world was a stark reminder of the rapidly approaching end of her own. She felt it pressing into her chest, a feeling not unlike a severe panic attack.

But before it had time to consume her, it was their turn at the reception window. She was so distracted by the feeling that it took a gently, prodding nudge from Jack to get her moving forward.

"Can I help you?" the receptionist behind the window asked. She seemed very cranky but was trying to mask it with some degree of professionalism. Rachel noted that she was wearing a light blue bandana over her head. From the looks of it, there was no hair underneath.

Rachel showed her badge and ID with a practiced fluidity that had come with years of making the motion. "Agents Gift and Rivers, FBI," she said.

"Hopefully here to send those protesters home?" the receptionist said, making the object of her frustration known.

"Actually, no," Rachel said. "We're looking into two murders that both seem to be leaning towards some sort of fertility link. We know for a fact that the first victim had been in touch with Regency. I'd like you to confirm that, if you can."

"Sure," the receptionist said. She no longer seemed irritated, but slightly unnerved. She nervously felt along the edges of the bandana, covering what Kate assumed was a bald head. "What's the woman's name?"

"Gloria Larsen."

The receptionist typed the name into her laptop and waited a moment. She then clicked her touchpad a few times and nodded. "Yes," she said. "I have her right here. In fact, Gloria Larsen was scheduled for her first appointment tomorrow at two in the afternoon."

"Does it say what the appointment was for?" Jack asked.

"Looks like just a few basic tests and to discuss potential treatment plans going forward."

"So she hadn't been here before?" Rachel said.

The receptionist did some more clicking and scrolling before eventually shaking her head. "No, it doesn't look like it."

"Would you mind taking a look for the name of the other victim? Her name is Lucinda Masters."

More typing, more clicking. "Yes, I see her here. She has an appointment scheduled for next week. From what I see here, she was set to begin her treatments."

Rachel and Jack shared a look. They'd just gotten a pretty unshakable link—one that might tie this whole case together. Rachel leaned in close and said, "I know there are hoops and logistics, but I really need a list of all women scheduled to receive fertility treatments in the next week or so."

The receptionist frowned and looked rather torn. "I'm sure you know, ma'am, that I can't just give out information like that. What I've already given you was probably too much. But women not involved in your case...I can't—"

"Who can make those decisions, then?"

Flustered, the receptionist shrugged. "Doctor Jergens is the lead doctor today. Maybe she could talk to you about it."

"I need you to buzz her, please. Agent Rivers and I will be over there," she said, nodding to the little farmhouse-decorated area.

They left the window and took a seat. Jack shook his head playfully and said, "You sounded pretty cut-throat with her."

Ignoring the comment completely, Rachel steepled her fingers in her lap and started working her way through what they knew. "A killer that is targeting women seeking fertility treatments is a bit specific, don't you think?"

"Yeah. The question then becomes if he's doing it because it's a fairly vulnerable population or because he feels *very* strongly about pro-life versus pro-choice."

"Doubtful," Rachel said, now sensing some of that cut-throat tone Jack had mentioned. "Someone concerned with the sanctity of life wouldn't take it so brutally."

"Not someone thinking logically, sure," Jack said.

Rachel looked back out to the reception windows. She eyed a couple holding hands as they walked to one of the windows. The fact that she and Peter had been trying to have a second child weighed on her. From trying to bring life into the world to being taken out of it in just a matter of hours...it was beyond jarring.

Rachel nearly started to brainstorm a bit more, but a woman in a generic doctor's smock came walking to them from the long hallway to the right of the receptionist windows. She looked hurried and annoyed—which was apparently a common theme today.

"I'm Dr. Jergens," she said. "I take it you're the FBI agents?"

"We are," Rachel said, getting to her feet.

"I've been informed that you want a list of women that are due for fertility treatments over the next week or so. But surely you understand I can't just give out that sort of personal information."

"I understand the principle of it, yes," Rachel said. "But two women have been murdered in a span of three days and this is the only link between them—and it's a very strong one. This is not coincidence. He's targeting the women because of their fertility treatments. I've been working these sorts of cases long enough to tell you with almost one hundred percent certainty that he'll do it again. I have no idea how he knows or how he's getting this information, but it seems he is."

"Still, there are rules and—"

Rachel lowered her voice and stepped closer to Jergens. "With all due respect, this killer doesn't give a damn about any rules. If I leave here without that list, I have no way of knowing who is next. And I'd rather you break some rules and give me the list now than have me back in here in a few days with a third body on our hands—a third name in your database. Would you give me this same argument then?"

The shift in Dr. Jergens' face told Rachel that she'd convinced her. But Jergens was not at all happy about it. "Wait here," she said. "I'll bring you your list. And I need you to sign a few papers if I'm handing over that sort if information."

"Of course."

Jergens stormed away and Rachel took her seat again. She was aware of Jack looking at her and waited for him to say something. As usual, he did not disappoint.

"Don't take this the wrong way," he said. "But you were sort of a bitch. Don't get me wrong…I kind of love it. But *yikes*."

She turned to him and she saw that he was smiling. They knew one another well enough for her to know not to take offense to his name calling. They'd certainly called each other worse in their few years together, and it was always in good fun.

"We're getting our list, aren't we?" she said. She meant for it to sound snarky, but it came out with an edge.

He nodded and looked at her with concern. "Hey…it's me, Rachel. Seriously, is everything okay?"

"Yeah," she said, the lie burning in her chest. "I think this case is just getting to me."

Jack dropped the subject and neither of them said another word until Jergens reappeared, walking down the hallway with their list in hand.

CHAPTER TWELVE

Back outside, the voices of the protestors seemed louder than they had going in. They came from behind poorly made signs and the collective cowardice of the group. Maybe it was just the stress of the day, or the faces of hopeful parents she'd seen inside, wanting to bring new life into the world. Whatever it was, the mere presence of the protestors annoyed Rachel. She did her best to look away from them as she and Jack returned to the car.

But as Rachel reached for the door handle on the driver's side, there was one woman's voice that seemed to rise over the rest of the din. It came hurtling toward Rachel as if the woman had thrown a spear at her, not an uninformed, stupid comment.

"So were the two of you in there opposing God's will, too?"

Rachel knew she should just get in the car and keep her mouth shut. But when her arm froze as she reached for the door handle, she knew it was too late. *God's will,* she thought. *I wonder if my doctor's appointment yesterday was part of God's will. What the hell do you know about God's will?*

"Not that it's any of your business," Rachel said, "but no."

Jack opened up his door on the passenger side and gave her a curious look—one that seemed to say: *Please don't engage these people.*

Undaunted, the same protestor stepped forward, dropping her little carboard sign to the ground. She pointed a beefy finger towards the clinic and said, "What they do in there is a direct violation of the will of our sovereign God! Freezing eggs and taking stem cells and—"

Rather than rolling her eyes and telling the woman to shut her mouth, Rachel instead pulled out her badge. She flashed at the woman as if she were brandishing a magic wand. "Back away from me, please," she said. "And do us both a favor: go home. What the people going in and out of this building might be dealing with is absolutely, one hundred percent none of your concern."

The woman and some of her friends eyed the badge and slowly stepped back a bit. Rachel noticed that one of the women slightly behind the presumed leader even lowered her sign and turned it around so that the blank side was showing. With that, Rachel finally got back into the car, swallowing down about five different further responses.

Jack also got in, closing his door and looking over to her as she cranked the car. "Well, that was fun," he said with a nervous grin. "Rachel, what the hell is going on?"

"Nothing," she said, trying not to bark at him. "I guess I'm just more irritable than usual."

He nodded and said, "And that's saying something."

But she knew he wasn't buying it; she knew he was worried about her, trying to determine how much pressure he should apply before backing off. Rachel gave the protestors one final glance in the rearview mirror as she pulled back out onto the street and headed in the direction of the local precinct.

* * *

The case felt pretty big to Rachel, so it confused her when the local PD only provided three additional officers for them to work with. Rachel and Jack stood at the front of a small conference room with three officers sitting at the table in front of them. She had elected to take the back seat for this meeting, not trusting the tumultuous wave of her emotions that had, so far, proven not to be very trustworthy today.

"Here's what we're dealing with," Jack said, placing the list of women from the clinic on the table. "We have a list of five women that look like they might be potential targets for this killer. Our job right now is to locate them. I'd prefer physical, face-to-face meetings, but if it has to be on the phone, we can deal with it. We need to make sure these women are not left alone until we find this killer. And even if they aren't alone, we need to keep eyes on them. The latest victim was at home, her husband upstairs and the killer got her anyway."

"What's the potential link between them all?" one of the men asked.

Jack quickly ran through the fertility treatments discovery and all three men seemed to grasp it and get on the same page right away. "I'll be coming out with you guys," Jack said. "Agent Gift, what's your preference?"

"I'll be on standby," she said. "I'll be looking into the clinic staff, but I'm also only a phone call away. This killer is striking quickly and without much hesitation. We have to assume he's planning another murder tonight."

Jack clapped his hands together and gave a knowing look of approval to the three officers. Sometimes Rachel was awed by how well he could connect with people; strangers tended to warm to him right away.

"Agent Gift and I tend to make meetings as fast as possible," he said. "So let's run these names, get addresses and phone numbers, and head out."

The officers did as asked, and Rachel could feel the dedication pretty much coming off of them, spurred by nothing more than a few words from Jack and a simple set of instructions. Jack made his way to the door, looking back at Rachel.

"You going to be okay by yourself for a bit?" he asked.

"Yes, I'll manage without you."

He gave her a sarcastic wink and headed out of the door. Standing in the conference room by herself, it was far too tempting to take one of the chairs and just zone out—to let the weight of the last twenty-four hours or so melt off of her. But she meant what she'd just told the officers—that based on the way this killer was behaving, they had so move as if they thought he would kill tonight as well.

She spent the next several minutes working with the receptionist of the precinct to procure a laptop, WiFi and internal server access, and a workspace. As all of that was being set up, Rachel placed a call to the clinic and, after a tense conversation with a manager and giving her badge number, got a full list of the staff members that worked at Regency Fertility Clinic. She hated the way she felt when she got off of the phone. Before this case was over, every single employee of that clinic was going to always be suspicious of the FBI or any other branch of law enforcement.

Working on a newer model of laptop at a cubicle near the back of what she supposed was meant to be the station bullpen, Rachel ran background checks on each employee. It took some getting used to the layout of the precinct's servers but it came pretty easily. When she was done about an hour and a half later, she'd discovered pretty much what she'd expected: exactly nothing. There were a few speeding tickets and one restraining order placed by one of the nurses, but nothing substantial.

When her options were exhausted, she looked to the list of names the clinic had sent over. Thirty-one employees, twenty-six of which were women. And while they all had squeaky clean records, that was not quite enough to sway Rachel's initial thought—that there might be an employee working with the killer, passing along the names of women getting these fertility treatments.

It was a terrible assumption to jump to, but it was the only thing that made sense so far. Besides, right now assumptions were all she had to work with. It was just one of the many ways the killer currently had a massive upper hand.

CHAPTER THIRTEEN

Rachel was digging through records for the past three years, looking for any cases in which pregnant women had been the target of crimes, when her phone rang. When she saw it was Peter, she almost ignored it. But she never ignored his calls unless she was in a position where her phone was on silent mode. She wasn't sure why her heart was pounding nervously when she answered it. Was keeping this secret from him going to cause her to feel this nervous and guilty every time they spoke?

"Hey, Peter," she answered.

"Hey yourself. You get there okay? Everything going fine?"

"Except for the nature of the case itself…yes, everything is fine."

This was something of a routine. He'd promised her early in her marriage that even when she became an active agent and was always on the road, he was going to check in on her, to let her know that someone was thinking about her back home. It had been a terribly romantic gesture back then but, from time to time, felt more burdensome than anything else. Still, she took it for what it was—a sign that he loved her deeply.

"Good. How's Jack?"

"He's Jack," she said. She knew she was sounding short, and tried to curb it. Apparently, Peter noticed, too, because he hurried up and got to the point.

"So, this is awkward," he said, "but I need to know for planning purposes. There's this massive edit we need to undertake on a proposal. It needs to go out tomorrow or our bid won't be accepted. I've told them I *might* be able to help. I had a look at the ovulation calendar and saw that tonight is a peak night. If you need my…er, *services* at home, I won't volunteer to help with the edit."

"If you're asking if this case is going to have me back home tonight, I'm sorry," she said. "There's not a single lead and it's…well, it's looking to be a very involved one. I'd guess three days at least."

"Oh."

He'd long ago gotten used to her sudden multiple day disappearances because of spur-of-the-moment cases and handled it like a champ. She did hear a bit of hurt in his single syllable response, though.

"I'm really sorry. I'll tell you the details when I can, when the case is wrapped—"

"No, really, it's okay. I didn't want to help with the edit anyway. The baby-making part, though…yeah, I'll miss that."

She couldn't come up with an appropriate response. She was suddenly back in Regency Fertility Clinic, seeing those hopeful faces and knowing that would never be her again…knowing she would likely not even be alive a year from now.

And then, like a ghost swooping into her mind, the face of Alex Lynch was in her head, smiling at her and studying her, his eyes magnified through his glasses.

What the hell is that about? she wondered.

"There's always next month," she said, finally, pushing that haunting face out of her mind.

"Yeah, but is there?" he said. It sounded a bit pained, and rather snappy.

"What's that supposed to mean?"

He sighed on the other end. "Nothing," he said. "I just…it doesn't seem like you're too interested, and *that* makes me feel like I'm pressuring you."

"Not at all," she said, sensing an argument right around the corner and trying to stave it off. "But we knew my schedule was going to play a part in how—and *if*—our plans worked out."

"I know," he said curtly. "This just…it just sucks."

She didn't know what to say. Just about anything would turn this into a full-fledged argument and that was not something she had time to deal with right now. Thankfully, Peter seemed to know this, too.

"I'll let you go. Sounds like you've got a big one on your hands."

"Thanks. I love you, Peter."

"Love you, too, Go get those bad guys."

He hung up with what had become almost like a tagline for him over the last few years when she was not at home. *Go get those bad guys.*

She looked to the list of staff members, wondering if any of any of them were the bad guys.

She was staring at the list for only a moment when someone approached her from behind. She turned to find Jack standing there, holding a Starbucks cup.

"Got you one of those green tea latte nonsense you like," he said, offering it to her.

"Thanks," she said, taking it gratefully.

"So, do you want me to pretend I didn't hear the last ten seconds or so of that conversation?"

"It doesn't matter. When sex isn't just about sex anymore—when you throw that whole baby-making business in, too—it becomes a really odd sort of minefield."

"He jealous of the job right now?"

"I don't think so. He's just pretty excited about the idea of another kid and it's like anything else in his life. He wants it, so he expects it now. The fact that I didn't get pregnant four months ago when we started trying really bothered him. And now, it's—"

She stopped here because what she wanted to mention next was how it was going to be even harder to tell him her most recent truth—the truth of why she knew a second child was not an option. Of course, if she'd told Jack about the cancer prognosis, she could get it out; she could word vomit all over him. But she'd kept the secret from him, and it now seemed like she'd made the right decision because being dealt such devastating news while now being involved on a case concerning fertility was a—

"Hold on," she said quietly. She took a sip from her green tea latte and sitting up straight.

"Yes?" Jack asked. "Has a lightbulb just gone off?"

"Maybe." She tapped the list of staff employees and said, "Maybe none of the clinic employees has a record, but maybe one of them does have another reason to loathe women who are looking to bring life into the world."

Jack looked at her with great curiosity from over the top of his own Starbucks drink. "Sorry," he said after he swallowed it down "I don't follow."

She checked her watch. It was 4:32….still enough time.

"Come on," she said, getting to her feet. "We're heading back to the clinic."

***

Rachel was pleased to see that the protestors had dispersed since they'd first visited the clinic. When they parked and walked inside, it was in the quiet of the afternoon. Rachel took the opportunity to relax herself, knowing that the line she was about to tread was a fragile one.

52

"You want to fill me in now?" Jack asked as he followed her across the lot.

"What do you remember about the receptionist we spoke to?"

He thought for a moment and said, "Not sure. Wasn't she wearing something over her head? Like a bandana or something?"

They were at the front door by then, so Rachel only nodded as she walked inside the clinic. Being that it was now the end of the day, there were no lines at the windows. Behind one of the windows, three women were speaking quietly. To the far left, Rachel saw the receptionist they'd spoken to before. She was typing something into her laptop but looked up to them when they approached. There was an initial look of confusion which she then tried to replace with a smile. Rachel barely noticed, though; she was eyeing the blue bandana on her head.

"Forget something?" the receptionist asked.

Rachel detected some anger. It made sense; they'd essentially tried pushing her to get them the list of names that she had fought against.

"No, we didn't forget anything," Rachel said. "But I was wondering if we could speak with you."

"With me? Why?"

"Just a few questions about the case. In private would be preferable."

"I don't understand what you need to speak with me about."

"Just a formality," Rachel said, already feeling rather bad about what was to come.

It was clear that the idea made her uncomfortable, but the receptionist leaned back in her chair and looked in the direction of the chatting women on the other side of the partition. "Hey, Giana, can you take my window for a second? I need to chat with these people."

She got up angrily and came around the partition. She nodded to the right, where there was a small waiting area. It was empty and already straightened up for tomorrow's business hours, the magazines all neatly stacked and the smell of disinfectant in the air. It was not a general waiting room, but the sort a patient might sit in while waiting for an outcome. For Rachel, it brought up images of her doctor's visit the day before and a chill passed through her.

"What's your name?" Jack asked as they all walked into the room. His voice was low and level. It was his way, Rachel supposed, of trying to fit into the scene. He was clearly confused—and that was Rachel's fault.

"Amber Seibert."

"Amber, how long have you worked here?" Rachel asked.

"This is year number eight."

"You like it?"

"I love it...most days. Of course, it's never fun when you are speaking with women that are learning they may never be able to have children."

"Forgive me for pointing this out," Rachel said, "but I couldn't help but notice the bandana." She took a breath, realizing she was about to cross a line. She was typically pretty good about knowing when to toe a line, but she felt a sense of urgency for this case that she was pretty sure was spurred on by her diagnosis. "Is it cancer? Are you taking chemotherapy?"

She was surprised when Amber didn't get angry. She just nodded and, almost with a bit of flair, took the bandana off to reveal her bald head. "Yeah. Chemo. I lost my hair, but I also lost about twenty-five pounds. I'd call it even." She grinned here, but there was no real humor in it.

"Did you miss a lot of time from work for the chemo?"

"Some. But everyone here has been very supportive, so there were no problems."

"Well, with your prognosis and having to deal with it all, it must have been difficult to come into work—to a place where you are around people trying to bring life *into* the world while you were fighting for your own, right?"

She could feel Jack shifting uncomfortably beside her, tensing up. In front of her, Amber cocked her head and looked quizzically at her. "No, not at all. In fact, I—"

The silence was deafening as she understood what was being asked of her. Slowly, a grim line of anger set across her mouth.

"Are you seriously suggesting that I...that...no. No, this is not only insulting, but an embarrassing breach of privacy."

"You have to understand where I'm coming from," Rachel said. "We are dealing with a killer that seems to have something against bringing life into the world that—"

"No!" Amber was to her feet now, glaring at them. "If you stop right now I'll consider not taking your names and contacting your supervisor. And not that it's any of your fucking business, but my day consists of coming to work and then heading home where I'm asleep by eight o' clock because the chemo treatments have wiped out any excess energy I might have. I might currently be in remission, but the draining nature of it sticks with you. I have my husband, my two children, and a neighbor that helps out that can back my story up."

"Amber," Jack said, just as shocked as she was. "We don't mean to—"

"Goodbye," she shouted as she walked through the door. "If I see either of you again, I *will* press charges."

She left the waiting area in an awkward silence. Jack got to his feet and looked out of the window that gave them a view of the edge of the parking lot. Without looking to Rachel, he said, "With all due respect, what in the hell was that all about?"

"Like I told her: someone is killing women based on their desire to bring new life into this world."

"And?"

"And the killer is getting the names *somehow*. What better place to look than a woman that works at the same clinic that has been staring death in the face?"

Saying it out loud, she realized how heartless it might have seemed. She also once again found herself on the verge of emotionally breaking at the mention of staring death in the face.

"Rachel, I know you well enough to know when something is wrong. You don't think like that. And even if you *did*, you'd talk it out first and you'd sure as hell have more compassion."

"Jack, I—"

"I don't know what's wrong with you," he said, finally turning to face her. "I don't know if it's the baby stuff with Peter, or something else. But I ask you as your partner and your friend to please get it together."

He looked to her for a moment and she was relieved to see more worry and compassion than outright anger in his eyes. He walked out without saying another word. Rachel got to her feet but she stood there in the silence a moment longer before she headed out after him.

CHAPTER FOURTEEN

Things were quiet in the car as they left the clinic. The few words that were spoken were all strictly related to the case—in deciding to check in with all of the units that were currently working to watch over the five names on the list for fertility treatments. As they made their way to the first address, she was again overcome with the need to tell Jack. But whenever she would start to form the words, a feeling of hopelessness would come over here. She sensed that coming clean with her prognosis would not draw a weight away from her shoulders, but would add on another. Did she really want to work with a partner that was always worrying about how she was feeling, thinking she might literally keel over at any moment?

She was wresting with this as she pulled her car in behind the police patrol car sitting outside the home of the first woman on the list. When she and Jack got out of the car to speak to the officer in charge of the check-in for this particular shift, there was still an icy sort of wall between them.

They approached the driver's side door, and the cop rolled his window down. "Hey, agents."

"Anything to report?" Rachel asked

"Not on my end, nope. Both the woman and her husband seemed grateful that we were taking precautions. Last I talked to the others, it's mostly the same. There was one lady—a Gena Reed—that was pissed because her husband didn't know she was taking the treatments. But I think that turned out well, too."

"Need any assistance?" Jack asked.

"No. We've got it all scheduled out. Sort of like miniature stakeouts around each home until this is wrapped up."

"Call us if any of that changes," Rachel said. "And if anything out of the ordinary should pop up."

The cop gave a satisfied nod and rolled his window back up. Rachel and Jack returned to their car and Rachel instantly pointed the car in the direction of the precinct.

"It was a good idea, in theory," Jack said out of nowhere.

"What?"

"Your hunch about Amber Seibert back at the clinic. But it should have been a discussion between us."

"I know. I'm sorry."

"I know you are. I can tell. As for me, *I'm* sorry I called you out. Yes, I do know you're dealing with something. I can tell that, too. But it's not my place to call you out on it. Just know that if there *is* something you're dealing with, I'm here for you."

Rachel could only nod and say, "Thanks." She feared saying anything else would bring on tears and, right behind them, the truth.

"Now, we can get back to the precinct, but it's nearing six o' clock and there are zero leads," Jack said. "Everything we need, we have digitally. I say we grab dinner and a beer, and call it a day."

They headed off to do exactly that as a fine mist of rain started to fall. The choice was an easy one—a little Mexican restaurant sitting right across the parking lot of the motel the bureau had booked for them. Even in the fifteen minutes that passed between leaving the officer on surveillance and pulling up a seat at the bar, Rachel once again felt the tension between them. The fact that she knew exactly where it came from made it so much worse. They ordered burritos and Coronas in the midst of that awkwardness. And it seemed to Rachel that the longer the silence persisted, the less she felt the need to share her secret with him.

She could not keep her mind from wandering back to the moment Dr. Greene had told her the news. Up until then, the biggest disappointment in her day had been her inability to beat the obstacle course time record. Jesus, how did something like *just yesterday* suddenly feel like it had happened years ago?

"We're decent friends, right?" Jack asked when he was nearing the bottom of his first beer. She was rather glad he'd decided to break the silence because she did not like where her thoughts had been headed. "Like, outside of the job, we're cool, right?"

"Yeah," she said, already knowing where he was going with it. That was one thing about Jack that could always be counted on: he was persistent to a fault.

"I think so, too. And with that in mind, I'm going to ask this and I'm only going to ask it once. "

"Jack..."

"Are you and Peter finding out that a new baby might not be in the cards? Because if that's the case, it makes a world of sense that this case would be affecting you the way it is. Hell, I'd even go to bat to have you taken off the case."

"That's not it," she said. Though, in a very roundabout way, she supposed it was at least *part* of it. Having a second kid was very much off the table, given that she wasn't expected to be alive in about a year's time.

"Okay," Jack said. He nodded, as if to say: *see, I just asked the one time and now it's dropped.* But that "okay" seemed to hold a lot more weight, and Rachel did not like the implication behind it.

"This case is just...it's landing at a very odd time for me," Rachel said.

"Okay. And that's your business. You apparently don't want to talk it out, so—"

"Why are you getting like this?"

"Me?" he asked, surprised. "It's *you* that's off-kilter and a little defensive."

"Believe it or not, Jack, there are some things in my private life that I prefer not to bring into work. I don't have to tell you everything."

"Yes, I know, Rachel. I know that, but—"

"Look, I'm very tired," she said, fishing into her wallet and dropping a twenty on the bar. "I'm going back to the hotel."

He looked taken aback, and she was afraid that she may have offended him. But in that moment, she didn't care. She left him staring as she walked away while the bartender brought him another drink.

***

As she'd fully expected, she felt guilty about the way she'd reacted the moment the door to her hotel room closed behind her. She also did not like the fact that the one beer she'd had seemed to be teasing her. Apparently, it was one of those days where one beer simply wasn't going to cut it. She toyed with the idea of heading out to a convenience store to grab a six pack but before she could act on it, her phone started ringing. She figured it would be Peter again and this annoyed her for reasons she did not understand or trust. She saw his name on the caller display and tried to hide her annoyance that it was a Facetime call. Still, she answered it.

When she saw Paige's face on the screen, smiling brightly, Rachel nearly burst into tears. She blinked them back at once and took a few steady breaths to keep herself under control.

"Hey, Mommy!" Paige said. She was the sort of kid that had not yet understood that you don't have to hold the phone right in front of your face, one inch from your nose to be seen on the other end. Most of what

Rachel saw was her daughter's mouth and nostrils. But her blue eyes peeked in from the side every now and then.

"Hey, sweetie! How are you?"

"I'm good. Daddy said it was okay to call. He's working late again, so Becka's still here."

"I know," Rachel said. "I'm so sorry neither one of us is there."

"It's okay. Me and Becka are gonna have a dance party after the call."

"Not for too long, I hope," Rachel said. She said it loudly, taking a dig at their usual sitter, Becka. She heard Becka chuckle in the background.

"I had a question about my birthday party," Paige said.

"But your birthday party isn't for another two months!"

"I know. But Becka said her little sister had this thing at her party and I thought it sounded cool. So, I was wondering if we could get a kroaky machine."

"A what?"

"A kroaky machine. You sing into it, and it has songs already on it."

"Oh. *Karaoke.*"

"Yeah, that."

Rachel had to wait a moment before she could respond. Paige would turn eight in two months. Where the hell had all the time gone? Knowing it would likely be the last birthday she would be able to celebrate with her daughter stung so deep it felt like someone had stabbed her in the heart with a blade of ice.

She wondered if the mention of any event from here on out was going to wreck her in a similar way. Every time a birthday or anniversary or trip that was more than a few months out…was she going to feel that her heart was shrinking at every single mention?

"Whatever you want, sweetie," Rachel said. And oh God, how she meant it.

"Thanks, Mommy. Hey, how long are you gonna be away?"

"I'm not sure. It's looking like at least two days or so. If it's more, I'll let you know."

"Okay. I love you! I'm gonna go dance now."

"Okay. I love you t—"

But Paige had already ended the call, lured by the promise of a two-person dance party. Rachel held the phone a bit longer, looking at the black screen and the words Call Ended. She wanted to throw the phone across the room. She wanted to scream. She wanted to call back to

Richmond and tell Director Anderson that she needed to quit her job and get the hell back home to her daughter as quickly as she could.

But she did none of those things. Instead, she decided to go out and get that six pack after all. She knew she wouldn't drink them all. Hell, she'd likely only get two down, if that. But it beat the hell out of staying in the room by herself. Besides, if she was going to start feeling sorry for herself, she'd at least like to have a couple of beers to place the blame on.

CHAPTER FIFTEEN

Hannah was angry at the security lights. Or, at least, that's what she was telling herself. She needed something to blame for her inability to sleep, so she might as well blame the glare of the security lights coming from the garage. They were new—just installed three weeks ago—and the glare cut even through the bedroom blinds.

She sat up in bed and looked to her phone, sitting plugged into its charger. It was 1:17 in the morning, and though she had gone to bed at 10:45, she'd slept for maybe half an hour and that had been a fitful sort of doze at best.

She could blame the security lights all she wanted, but she knew the real reason she couldn't sleep. She couldn't sleep because she was nervous about the fertility treatments she was going to be getting tomorrow. If they later found out the treatments had done no good, then she and her husband would have to face the fact that they were never going to be able to have biological children.

She almost reached over and shook Ryan awake. She would ask him to pray with her, to help sooth her and calm her nerves. He'd been praying about the treatments tomorrow just as much, if not more, than she had and he'd be more than happy to be there for her. But there was no sense in both of them losing sleep over this.

And now that she had spent almost two and a half hours in bed awake, her stupid stomach was insisting that it was hungry. She knew to lay there and ignore it would only make her angrier, so she didn't bother. She slid out of bed and quietly left the upstairs bedroom. As she walked to the stairs, she passed by the room that they hoped would one day be the nursery and her guts suddenly felt as if they'd been dropped down a canyon.

She went downstairs and plodded into the kitchen. She was tired and she was mad that she was tired, and it all just…well, it all just *sucked.* She went to the fridge and got out some of the leftover chicken from dinner. She then took out a string cheese and walked to the table. She was unwrapping the string cheese and lowering her butt into a chair at the table when she saw a flicker of movement outside of the kitchen window.

Her first reaction was fright. It was, after all, in the dead of night and the house was deathly quiet. But then she remembered some of the posts she'd seen on the neighborhood Facebook page. People had been posting pictures of the deer that had started wandering in from the rural areas outside of the city. It was certainly strange to see deer in Baltimore, even in the more rural areas, but the Facebook pictures had proven it was real. Apparently, they were eating some people's bushes and roses. Some very uppity people on the Facebook page were asking if the POA should get involved, or maybe even the game warden

Hannah thought all of that was just a bit much, though. Thinking she might get her own sighting, she hurried to the back door. She quickly disarmed the alarm, which went active after ten p.m. and walked out to the back porch. She looked around the yard and didn't see a deer—or anything else that would have caused a blur of motion through the window. She then thought that if there *was* as deer, it had likely moved to the side yard to snack on her azalea bushes. She smiled as she thought of how she might sarcastically bemoan such an atrocity on the neighborhood Facebook page.

She hurried quietly down the porch stairs, not wanting to spook the deer. Passing through the grass in the quiet of the night in her bare feet was pleasant in a way she had not expected. It made her feel like a kid again, like she was sneaking around and getting into mischief.

She came to the edge of the house and there it was. A shape in the darkness, against the side of the house.

Hannah discovered that it wasn't a deer just a moment too late.

By the time she recognized that the shape was very much human, there was a hand clamped around her mouth and a knife slamming into her ribs.

CHAPTER SIXTEEN

When Rachel's phone rang, stirring her awake, she was coming out some half-remembered dream that had featured the peering eyes of Alex Lynch, looking at her as if she were a specimen under a microscope. When she reached for the phone, Rachel was certain it was going to be the doctor's office calling to tell her that they'd misread her results and that there was no tumor after all.

Sorry for the mix-up. Whoops. Our bad.

But then she realized she was not in her bedroom, but a motel room. And then reality came flooding back and she loathed her phone for making her face it all again. She did not recognize the number, but knew it was a Baltimore area code. She also noted that it was 5:02 in the morning. With a bad feeling already forming in her guts, she answered it. She tried not to sound tired and discombobulated, but failed miserably.

"This is Agent Gift."

"Agent Gift, this is Sergeant Owen. We met at the Masters' residence earlier today."

"Another one?" she asked.

The silence was answer enough but after several quiet moments, Owen answered in a shaky voice. "Yeah."

Rachel grabbed the hotel room stationery from the bedside table and a pen from the drawer. "The address?"

He gave it to her and she scribbled it down. Ending the call, Rachel slid out of bed and started to get dressed. As she slid into her pants, her mind instantly brought up memories of being in the doctor's office, of getting the bad news. She wondered if it was just going to be this huge, mental juggernaut and if it would keep stalking her even after she'd come clean with it. Was this her life now, defined totally by this one bit of terrible news?

Shaking the thoughts away, she called Jack's number. He answered on the fourth ring and, like Rachel, made very little attempt to sound as if he had not just been stirred awake far too early.

"It's barely after five in the morning," he croaked.

"I know. But I just got a call."

Again, his response echoed hers from moments ago. "Another one?"

"Yeah."

"Even with the cops keeping look-out?"

"Seems that way," she said, confused over the matter herself.

"I'll meet you at the car in three minutes."

***

It started to make a dark sort of sense when they arrived at the crime scene. It was the residence of Hannah and Ryan Kettleman. It was nearly on the opposite side of town from the other two murders. But most significant of all was the fact that Hannah Kettleman had not been a name on the list they'd gotten from Regency Fertility Clinic.

As Rachel and Jack walked around the side of the house to where several police were gathered, it all started to feel similar. A murder in the back yard, just like Lucinda Masters. That was almost enough to kill off any hope Rachel had that the murder might be unrelated. But when they saw the body and the grim looks on the faces of the gathered officers, it died away completely.

She recognized Owen from the Masters' residence and approached him right away. "She's not on the list we got from the clinic."

"I know," Maters said. "All the same, the husband tells us that she was scheduled for fertility treatments tomorrow."

"But how—"

"It's a different facility. Not Regency."

Rachel nodded as she and Jack approached the body. Forensics, who had just pulled in ahead of them, were also closely studying the body. She heard their murmured conversation as they took notes and confirmed everything they said with her own eyes. It looked exactly the same as the first two victims: multiple stab wounds in the abdomen area, done in a fashion that seemed hurried and urgent. On this new victim, there was a slash lower than all the rest, nearly in the groin, but it was slanted upward, indicating the knife used to do the stabbing had slipped.

Yet again, Rachel's thoughts went to Alex Lynch. He'd killed with similar brutality, almost as if he'd enjoyed it—had *thrived* on it. And while the similarity was enough to bring his case to mind, she hated that she felt so drawn to his old case because of this new one. She'd spent so much time trying to forget about him, spending months in therapy. Now she felt like she was taking several steps back, letting that vile man back into her mind.

"Where's the husband?" Jack asked.

"He's inside with the EMTs," one of the officers said. "He gave is information like a champ for about two minutes and then it all hit him. He's being treated for shock."

"Jesus, I guess so," Jack said. "Did he have anything to share that would be useful?"

"No. Poor guy is floored. I honestly don't even think he's fully aware of what has happened."

The crime scene then fell into a silence Rachel had seen before—everyone realizing that they were standing in the middle of a huge event, in the shadow of evil. The man that had done this was sick, that was for sure. But as Rachel looked to the body and stepped aside to let the forensics team get in closer, her mind shifted into some other place. It seemed to be doing that a lot lately—perhaps in response to her sudden rampant thoughts and memories of Alex Lynch.

"What if it's not just about the fertility treatments?" she wondered out loud.

"What do you mean?" Jack asked.

"I mean the fertility treatments are a definite link. There's no question about that. But he's also killed them the same way every single time. They're all at home. The wounds are all in the stomach or sides angling into the abdomen. It's always with a knife and there's nothing neat or precise about it. Maybe there's something we can use in that…in the *way* he's doing it."

"I'm not sure that sort of answer would help us, either," Jack said.

Rachel looked back over to the cops and asked: "Did anyone ask the husband about security footage before he went into shock?"

"Yeah. They've got cameras at the back of the garage and a Ring doorbell front door, but nothing back here. There's an alarm on the back door, but he says it was disengaged. He figures she disengaged it when she walked outside."

"Has anyone checked the Ring footage?"

"We did. There's nothing. A single car goes by but we obviously can't see the plate."

"Any idea why she might have come outside in the first place?" Jack asked.

"We didn't get that far," Owen said.

Rachel paced around the back yard. She looked to the garage, where halogen security lights glared. She scanned the yard and looked back to the body. Something wasn't adding up here. As she stood there, the first true light of dawn crept across the Kettleman's back yard but it felt almost melodramatic. Light or not, there were no leads or clues here. The lights, the layout of the yard…it made her think this was a calculated killer. He'd planned it and plotted it. He'd likely driven by the houses of his victims to study the layouts, to learn their schedules. And given how quickly he was working, it likely meant he'd been very meticulous. He knew their names, their addresses, details of their houses and schedules from the looks of it. This could get very bad, very soon.

"Earth to Rachel," Jack whispered. "You okay?"

Rachel thought of Paige being at home with a babysitter. She thought of her diagnosis and how, at some point, she was going to have to come clean with it. She thought of not being there for her daughter, leaving her husband to raise a child by himself. Slowly, in the light of a new morning, the pity she had caught a glimpse of last night turned to something else. It started to turn into anger.

"No," she said. "This case is starting to piss me off."

"The *case* or the killer's actions?"

"Both. I say we find out where this woman was supposed to be getting her treatments and start there. All over again, like yesterday. Two clinics, three dead women…someone has got to know *something.*"

CHAPTER SEVENTEEN

They arrived at the clinic fifteen minutes before business hours. It was called Greenfield Women's Health Services and was about half the size of Regency. The doors were still locked with they approached but some sturdy knocking eventually got a very flustered-looking nurse to come to the door.

Though a small crack in the double doors, the fifty-something woman looked to them with disapproving eyes. "We don't open for another fifteen minutes," she said.

"I know, and I'm sorry," Rachel said, showing her badge. "But I was really hoping to speak to someone before you officially opened for the day. We're with the FBI and are looking into a series of murders."

"Oh," the woman said. "Oh, well yes, please come in. I'll get Mrs. Carpenter, the manager for you."

She opened the door for them and ushered them in before hurrying to a small reception area directly ahead of them. One other receptionist was already at work, speaking on the phone while typing something into a laptop. The woman that answered the door for them grabbed up the landline phone and typed in an extension. She spoke hurriedly into the phone for a moment and looked to them with great urgency.

"Mrs. Carpenter is on her way," she said.

Rachel and Jack stood against the wall as Rachel compared the approach of this clinic to Regency. Even now, before the doors officially opened, the people here seemed eager to help. At Regency, there had been a lot of hesitancy and even something resembling annoyance. Of course, in the space of the day that had passed, Rachel figured news of the murders had spread and now the matter was being taken more seriously. She just hoped that carried over in speaking to the manager.

She met them two minutes later. Dressed in a stylish pantsuit, Mrs. Carpenter approached them with the same sense of urgency the receptionist had shown. She looked to be roughly middle aged, with the sort of thin smile that looked like it was pretty much always on her face.

"Good morning, agents," she said. "Emma tells me you're here to talk about those awful murders. What can I do to help?"

"You've heard about them already?" Jack asked.

"Yes. It was brough to our attention yesterday through a Facebook post from a concerned pregnant woman. Of course, I'm sure you know that neither of the victims was a patient here."

"The first two weren't," Rachel said. "But there was a third last night and her husband has confirmed that she was due to come here today for fertility treatments."

"Oh my God," Carpenter said. "What...what was her name?"

"Hannah Kettleman."

"One moment, please," Carpenter said, scurrying over to the receptionist she'd identified as Emma. Rachel heard her ask Emma for the records for a patient by the name of Hannah Kettleman. Thirty seconds later, she was walking back over with a smart pad. She stood between them and let them see the screen.

"Hannah Kettleman, thirty-six years old. She had an appointment scheduled for 10:30 this morning. Right here, you can see where she had been here two previous times for tests to find out if she was a viable candidate for treatments."

"No other appointments in the past?" Jack asked.

Carpenter scrolled a bit and shook her head. "Just gynecological check-ups."

"Mrs. Carpenter, this is three women in three days," Rachel said. "And so far, there are zero leads. I hope you understand that were having to take drastic measures to find this killer. That being said, I need a list of women that are scheduled for treatments over the next few weeks."

She was expecting push-back so she was pleasantly surprised when Carpenter nodded enthusiastically. "Of course, I can get that for you right away."

"And staff members as well," Jack said, almost apologetically.

At this, there was some skepticism. "Why's that?" Carpenter asked, raising an eyebrow.

"You have to understand that the main point of confusion comes from how this killer knows these women are getting treatments."

"And because the victims are all linked by this one factor," Rachel said, "we have to start at the most obvious conclusion: that someone at these clinics is leaking the information. We've already done background checks on everyone at Regency and they've come out clean."

"And so will ours," Carpenter said defiantly. "So yes, I'll get you a list of names for staff members, too. Give me just a few minutes, would you?"

Carpenter left them alone again. Jack sighed and cracked his knuckles nervously—a little nervous tic of his that Rachel actually found calming. "You know," he said, "it didn't truly hit me until I heard it out of your mouth just now. Three victims in three days. And if he's got some sort of a leaked list...fuck. We're in deep here."

It was rare that Jack got flustered, and even rarer that he dropped an f-bomb around her. "I mean...do we think about putting out a citywide alert for all women that are scheduled for fertility treatments?" he said.

"That would never fly. It brings up privacy issues. I'm starting to think along those extreme measures, too, though. I wonder if it might be plausible to have every clinic dealing with fertility treatments to be temporarily shut down until we find our killer."

"That could work," Jack said. "But the mere act of getting that approved would likely take days. And at the rate this killer is moving..."

He didn't need to finish his statement for his point to be made. As they stewed in these ideas, Mrs. Carpenter came back to them with several sheets of paper. She had already separated the papers for them and made a point of showing them so.

"This," she said, handing Jack two stapled sheets of paper, "is a list of every women due to come in for treatments in the next month. There are eight in all. And this," she said, handing Rachel four sheets stapled together, "is a list of our staff, complete with phone numbers, email addresses, and home addresses. I do ask that if you need to actually contact one of them that I would be notified."

"Of course," Rachel said. "Thank you so much."

"I'm glad to help. However, there is one thing that you should know...and it pretty much proves the innocence of my entire staff, if I may be so blunt."

"What one thing is that?" Rachel asked.

"Even if there *is* someone leaking these names, the fact that the killer is now targeting women from two clinics complicates things. If it were someone on my staff, they would not have access to a list of women receiving treatments from another clinic. We simply don't share that information with other clinics—or anyone outside of agencies like yours."

Damn, Rachel thought. *How did I miss that?*

"Of course," Rachel said.

"Is there anything else?" Carpenter asked. "We have exactly three minutes before we have to open the doors for the day."

"No thank you. You've been a tremendous help."

Rachel and Jack slipped out as Mrs. Carpenter unlocked the doors to start the clinic's day. Rachel was thrilled to have the lists, but based on the glaring observation Carpenter had made about not being able to share information with other clinics, she wasn't sure how much good it would do.

"Man," Jack said as they neared the car. "These people start early, I see."

Rachel looked ahead and saw a small group of protestors beginning to gather together at the edge of the parking lot. A brief glance was all the attention she gave them. She really didn't need another reason to get annoyed this morning. She had to get hyper-focused on the case.

She got behind the wheel, cranked the car, and was about to pull off when she saw something that triggered a flash of familiarity.

She pointed to one of the women and said, "Jack, does that woman look familiar to you?"

Jack looked to the woman in question and shrugged. "Not sure. I don't think so."

"She was at Regency yesterday. She was the one that called us out when we were leaving—the one that thought we'd gone in together as a married couple." Rachel looked out again, just to be sure. And yes, it was the same woman—the same dark shoulder-length hair, the same glasses, the same angry-looking fixed stare.

Jack looked again and recognition spread across his face. "Yeah, that *is* her."

"Seems she stays busy with these protests, huh?"

"It does. And to show up at the two that are centered around the killings…I think that at least warrants some questioning."

Rachel killed the engine and got out. Jack joined her and they walked slowly to the other side of the lot, the one directly by the little two-lane feeder road that connected the parking lot to the busier streets beyond. The group consisted of only seven people so far and most of them noticed the two people headed their way.

"Excuse me," Rachel said as she approached. The woman they had recognized looked up. There was irritation on her face at first, presumably thinking her little group was about to get lectured. But then she seemed to recognize Rachel and her eyes went wide with worry.

"Yeah, you," Rachel said, pointing her out with a rigid index finger. "You stay busy with this stuff, huh? Funny seeing you here this morning."

"I have a right to protest," the woman said, though there was little defiance in her voice.

"You do," Rachel conceded. "You're absolutely right. But, as an FBI agent, I also have a right to question you about why you were at one clinic yesterday and another today—both of which just happen to be at the center of a case my partner and I are working on."

"Question *me?*" she asked.

"Yes. And it'll be a lot less awkward if you step away from your friends there and—"

The woman did exactly that. Only when she did, she took off running in the opposite direction. She ran for the feeder road, away from Rachel and Jack at an angle and to the scattered buildings beyond.

"Are you freaking kidding me?" Rachel asked, taking off after her.

She was barely aware of Jack chasing behind her. For a moment, she was back on the training course, trying to destroy her time. And with anger and adrenaline pumping through her in equal measure, this woman that seemed to have a passion for protesting was soon going to find out just how much of a mistake it was to try running from Agent Rachel Gift—and Jack was going to be reminded just how hard it was to keep up.

CHAPTER EIGHTEEN

The ironic thing about the whole scene was that for as far back as she could remember, Rachel had liked to run. She'd done some cross country in high school, a couple of marathons during college, and tried to get in at least three runs of three miles or more a few times a week. And when she found herself running during work—which did not happen very frequently—it was hard not to see it as a competition.

Rachel saw the protestor in front of her, and she was closing in fast. Most panicked people did not understand how stupid it was to try running from the police or any other arm of the law if they themselves were not used to running. It was just something that a panicked nervous system insisted was the best thing to do. Still, it felt like a sport to Rachel, and she *almost* considered slowing down a bit to allow the protestor a bit more room—to allow the chase to go on for a few more seconds. It was a juvenile response, sure, but every now and then her competitive nature reared its head even in these situations.

They'd crossed the little feeder road and were now running across a back parking lot, used for loading and unloading as well as employee parking. Rachel could hear Jack padding along behind her and she was sure he'd give her an earful when this was over, but—

All thought came to a sudden halt as a bolt of light flashed across her vision. It was accompanied by a dull ache that seemed to radiate all the way across her head. Again, she was back at the training course, staggered by the flashing light and pain.

She gasped, let out a little moan and then her knees buckled. She managed to stay mostly upright for a moment rather than falling flat out on her face. Instead, she slowly dropped to the ground on her knees and slowly bent over as if she were having a severe stomach cramp. Again, the light came, dull and flickering this time.

Is this it? she wondered. *By pushing myself did I shorten my year or so to just a handful of days? Is this how I'm going out?*

But even by then, the pain seemed to be fading. There was one final flicker of that white light across her field of vision, and then it seemed to be gone. The ground felt like it was swaying a bit beneath her as Jack finally reached her. He stopped and knelt down by her.

"What's wrong?" he asked, panting. There was an extreme look of worry on his face. It made sense, she supposed; she wasn't sure he'd ever seen her injured or in any sort of weakened state.

"Don't know. Pulled something." The lie came so easily that it made her feel absolutely awful. "Just go get her…"

Jack brought her lie and took off right away. Rachel remained there for a moment and slowly got back to her feet. She took one experimental step and then another. She was still wobbly and wasn't going to be running again anytime in the next few minutes, that was obvious. She walked slowly over to the back stoop of what looked to be a small packaging business and sat down. She focused on her breathing, tried to clear her mind, and did her best to keep the wave of emotion she could feel from crashing and obliterating everything.

She could just barely hear the sounds of the footrace between Jack and the protestor. Their footfalls were like little blasts of thunder from a great distance. After a few seconds, she heard the protestor give a cry of despair, followed by Jack's murmured voice. Hearing all of this, Rachel forced herself to her feet and walked in the direction of the commotion. The protestor had led Jack down a thin alleyway between two buildings, cluttered with broken down cardboard boxes and waste bins. When Rachel spotted them, Jack was gently pulling the woman up to her feet. He'd already cuffed her and the woman's face was locked in an odd expression; it seemed that she was trying to decide if she should be pissed off or scared.

"All good?" Rachel asked. She made sure not to move or speak too fast. She had no idea what sort of movements might trigger another episode. At the same time, though, she did her best to appear normal.

"Yeah, we're good," Jack said.

"You think so?" the protestor asked. "You just wait until I call my lawyer."

"I'll do that," Jack said. "Maybe he can tell us why you decided it would be a smarter bet to run from us than answer some questions. I'd *love* to hear how that goes."

The three of them walked back across the lot and feeder road. The protestor did not argue or put up much of a fight. She did, however, receive a smattering of applause from the other protestors when they arrived back at the car. A few of the protestors cast curse words and threats at Rachel and Jack, but neither of them took the bait. With the runaway protestor in the back of the car, Rachel got behind the wheel and pulled out of the lot.

"You sure you're okay?" Jack asked.

"I think so. I think I just did too much, too fast."

"You understand why I find that hard to believe, right? You're always in amazing shape and I've seen you hustle a lot harder than that in the past with no issues."

She felt a sting of irritation coming on, but squashed it right away. She grinned, still playing a part, and said: "Yeah, well, I guess aging is just a bitch, huh?"

Jack grinned back, nodding, but it was clear that he was not totally convinced. But if he suspected something, he said nothing about it and for that, Rachel was thankful.

***

Her name was Maria Oliver, she was a forty-three year-old divorcee and she lived in Baltimore. Rachel and Jack were able to get these small details out of her on the way back to the station. Other than that, though, she spent a lot of time griping about her rights being infringed upon and how fertility clinics were trying to play God.

Slowly, as they got closer to the station, Maria Oliver started to calm down. Rachel had seen it countless times before—the criminal acting angry and aghast that they were being arrested, screaming and fighting at first but then slowly becoming subdued as they got closer to the station and the reality of the situation came over them. Maria was no different. It was like a little puppy placed in a crate, yelping and whining hard for the first few minutes but quiet and accepting several minutes later.

Once she calmed down, Rachel tried to get a little more information out of her, thinking she was likely coming around to the acceptance phase of things. "Is there anyone we can call for you to let them know what has happened?"

"No," Maria barked from the back. She then chuckled nervously and said, "You realize you just made me a hero, right? To all of the women I protest with…this is only going to make them admire the cause even more."

"Well, I guess that all depends on how the next few hours go for you," Jack said.

"I've done nothing wrong! It's my God-given right to protest!"

And any woman's God-given right to look into fertility treatments if they have no other alternative when it comes to having a baby, Rachel thought. She kept it to herself, however. She was starting to feel a very dangerous sort of irritation towards this case in general—toward a

74

killer that seemed to be targeting women intent on doing what they could to have a baby.

The rest of the trip to the station was silent. Other than a few deep sighs and frustrated exhales from the back, Maria remained quiet. They escorted her into the building without incident and when they had her sitting in an interrogation room, they wasted no time. Perhaps sensing the growing tension in Rachel, Jack did his best to play the good cop, bringing Maria a cup of tea when they entered to speak with her.

Rachel had Maria's file in her hand and it revealed nothing surprising. She'd been arrested one other time, two years ago, for being involved in a protest that got out of control. Other than that, though, her record was squeaky clean. Rachel knew this did not clear the woman at all, but it *did* make her job a bit harder.

"I ask this not out of spite, but admitted ignorance," Rachel said. "As far as we know, neither of the clinics we spotted you at perform abortions. Can you tell us what, exactly, you were protesting?"

Maria looked to Rachel like she'd just asked an incredibly stupid question. "I'm protesting the idea that human beings think they know better than God."

"I'm going to need you to explain a bit better than that," Rachel said.

"If God makes it so that people can't have children, that's that. He is sovereign and knows what He's doing. Getting a doctor to manipulate your womb or a man's semen is blasphemy. Fertility treatments are an afront against an all-knowing Creator and are an abomination."

Hearing Maria say this, Rachel was almost alarmed that she understood it. She did not *agree* with it, but it was easy to track. Of course, Rachel did not care for hearing anything about a sovereign creator of a God. It was apparently a God that also slipped in a tumor from time to time—to people that had been healthy up until that point. If that was the same God Maria was spouting on about, he was sort of an uncaring jerk. Rachel focused on this feeling for a moment, but only to identify. She could not allow it to alter the way she questioned this woman or things were going to get nasty.

"So based on such beliefs," Rachel said, "I would assume you would agree with me that people should not murder, right?"

"Correct," Maria said proudly. "Abortion is a—"

"No, not abortion," Rachel interrupted. "I'm talking about straight out murder."

"Same thing. It's right there in the Ten Commandments. Thou shalt not murder."

"I take it you try to abide by the rules and regulations of the Bible, right?" Rachel said.

Maria leaned forward, clearly getting irritated. "We are all fallen. Even the purest of humans is a sinner. We all fall short of God's glory. I have flaws. I've made mistakes. I'm a sinner just like you. Just like *everyone.*"

Jack could apparently tell that she was struggling to keep a civil tongue. He spoke up before she could and even *his* response was layered with subtle ridicule. "Are some of the sins you've committed perhaps behind the reason you thought it would be a good idea to run away from us today? If you were legitimately just protesting, I find it hard to believe you'd have any reason to get into a race with federal agents."

Maria almost answered right away but them smirked at them. "You really think you're going to lure me into that trap?"

"Here's the deal," Rachel said, now taking her turn to lean forward a bit. "I'm going to tell you what's going on since you seem to take this whole 'though shalt not murder' thing so seriously. We are looking for a killer. We are looking for someone that has taken to killing women that are scheduled for fertility treatments. Three so far. Now, in the course of our searching, we have been led to two different clinics. And both times we have been to those clinics, we have seen *you.* That is why we approached you today. So now...how about it? How about *now* you tell us why you ran?"

Maria looked absolutely shocked. She tried to answer on two different occasions, but the words seemed to get hung in her throat. She slowly started to shake her head, whether in denial of the news itself or to signify that she had not done it. Rachel watched every movement of her head, every tic or twitch of the tics around her mouth. She wasn't sure she believed the shock on the woman's face but from a simple glance, it *did* appear to be genuine.

"Three nights ago," she said slowly. "I was with some other protestors late at night. There was this other clinic...the one downtown that's basically Planned Parenthood. It was just some spray-paint and bricks. We didn't hurt anyone, though. Not a single person."

Jack sighed and said, "You ran because you thought we were going to question you about that?"

"Yes, I swear it."

Rachel wasn't quite sure if she was telling the whole truth or not. But what she did know, though, that their first victim was being killed three nights ago. "Ms. Oliver, if we give you three specific times, would you be able to prove your whereabouts?"

"It depends on the nights and how late. I tend to go to sleep somewhat early."

"When you aren't defacing public buildings, you mean?" Rachel asked.

The comment seemed to have gone mostly unheard by Maria. Jack followed up, keeping things professional in the wake of Rachel's cynicism. "If we have trouble proving your whereabouts and need your phone to help prove where you were at any given time, would you concede to handing it over?"

"What nights?"

"For instance, how about Tuesday night? Where were you?"

"Tuesday, I was at a friend's house and I drank far too much wine. I had to take a cab home. I can show you credit card receipts for it if you need me to."

It was a huge move in Maria's favor, and it felt like a blow straight to Rachel's heart.

"Can you provide similar proof of any other night?" Jack asked.

"Yes," Maria said. "But if it's any time after eleven or so, it's going to consist of me at home, sleeping." Something like clarity seemed to slowly fall over her as she looked directly to Rachel. "I swear, I would never kill anyone. I only protest these things because I want to keep God's natural design in place. And murder like what you're talking about...that was never part of God's natural design."

Rachel nodded and got to her feet. "Thank you. We'll send officers in to corroborate your whereabouts on the night of each murder. If your alibis are tight, you're free to go."

As Rachel reached the door, Maria Oliver called out in a voice that was shaky and near tears. "I really am sorry I ran," she said. "I was feeling very guilty about taking part in messing up that building. If I'd known what you were really looking for, I would not have wasted your time."

Rachel nearly walked out without even acknowledging this comment. But knowing that she was being purposefully rude was only making her even angrier with herself. Yes, she kept telling herself that she would not feel sorry for herself but at the root of it all, that's basically what was going on. She was throwing a little tantrum because the God that Maria Oliver so firmly believed in had dealt her a shitty hand.

She said nothing, but did manage to give Maria a nod of acknowledgement without coming off as nasty. She stepped out into the hallway, feeling as if she'd just dodged a bullet. Another few moments in there with Maria and she thought she may have ended up saying something that would have been considered "too far." And the last thing she needed was for to Jack to have one more thing to add to his pile of ammo the next time he asked if there was something going on with her.

Jack stepped out a few seconds later, closing the door softly and quietly behind him. She was almost certain he was going to ask what was wrong—what was bothering her so badly. Instead, he simply sighed and sagged against the wall.

"Initial thoughts?" he said.

"It's doubtful it's her. That, or she's an Academy Award-level actress."

"Her willingness to hand her phone over for location services is what did it for me," Jack said. He had taken out his own phone and was typing something into it. "It certainly wasn't going all holy-roller preacher and telling me how everyone is a sinner." He said this as he started scrolling through something on his phone.

"What are you looking for?" she asked.

"Checking local news to see if we can at least verify a clinic that has been defaced recently. Maybe I'll check Facebook or social media posts with that specific search to find it if the local news reports aren't' enough."

It all registered for Rachel right away, but one particular nugget stuck out. "Social media," she said.

"What about it?"

"Maybe that's how the killer was finding the women," she said, the idea suddenly seeming brighter and brighter by the moment. "Maybe there's no leak…maybe he's just really dedicated and knows where to look on social media."

Jack looked up to her, smiling as the idea of it fully ensnared them both. And then, without a single word spoken between them, they hurried to their workspace in the back of the building, already pulling up Facebook on their phones. They had a potential lead and, as was becoming more and more the case within the bureau, something as simple as social media may very well provide the answer.

CHAPTER NINETEEN

It was a peculiar feeling that Rachel wasn't sure she would ever get used to, and it had settled over her like a veil in the two hours following their initial interrogation of Maria Oliver. Over the past several years, it had become commonplace for a lot of research work to be conducted on social media. Rachel had personally spent hours on Facebook and Instagram, tracking the movements and chatter of suspected killers and small-town terrorists over the last three years or so. She *knew* such digging was becoming more and more effective, but it still sometimes felt like she was doing little more than goofing off on social media.

"Okay, so I've got two links between Gloria Larsen and Lucinda Masters," Jack said, sitting on the edge of the tiny desk. "The first is that they both like Trader Joe's. The second is a mutual friend by the name of Wendy Timmons. Looking at Wendy's profile and some of her posts, though, I think it might just be a single, common shared friend from a local gym."

Rachel jotted down the name Wendy Timmons and then went back to her own search. She found that Lucinda Masters had been a member of lots of Facebook groups—like *a lot*. She was a "fan" of at least twenty pages for various television shows, from a *Friends* fan group to a True Crime on Netflix group. She followed different chain stores, several celebrities, and local businesses, too.

She fished through them all, getting a rather widespread look into Lucinda's life. It was both informative and creepy to be peering through the interests of a dead woman in such a digital and impersonal way. It paid off, though. In her search, she found two groups that jumped out to her. One was called Family Focus Fertility and the other was Baby Blues. She scribbled these down as well and then checked the profiles of Gloria Larsen and Hannah Kettleman. She wasn't expecting much, as she could only imagine how many groups there were out there to help support and encourage women that were having trouble getting pregnant.

Yet it took less than a minute to find a connection. She double-checked just to make sure she was seeing it right and then sat forward at the small desk. "This could be pretty big," she said, showing her phone to Jack. "All three of our victims were members of a Facebook group called Family Focus Fertility."

"That *could* be big," Jack said. "How many members?"

"Just over three thousand. And that tells me that three women, all in the same city, being a part of it…"

She left the comment unfinished, but Jack picked up. "If someone *was* targeting local woman looking into fertility treatments, this was basically a roadmap of how to get to them. I mean…is the group a public or private group?"

"Public. And right here, I'm looking at a post from Hannah Kettleman from eight days ago. She's asking for prayers and encouragement because her first treatment is right around the corner. There are thirty-seven comments. And just randomly clicking through the people that commented, I've got one from Texas…one from Hawaii, one from Maine. These people are all spread out."

"Except our three victims," Jack said. "But the fact that this thing is a public page…there's very little chance it will actually turn out to help us at all."

"That's true," Rachel agreed. "But I think it's a safe bet that this would be a very likely resource for the killer to hunt down these women. We know how he's finding them, anyway."

"So do we just go through this group woman by woman to see if there are any other in the immediate area?"

"Within twenty-five miles, at least."

She said this with some distance, her thoughts starting to stray slightly away from the conversation. She could picture somehow scrolling through Facebook just like she was, locating their next victim with ease through groups like this. The next question then became: *why?* There could be countless answers to this, but she was leaning more toward something very similar to the sort of diatribe they'd just heard from Maria Oliver. But no…Rachel was quite sure there were no religious motives here. There wasn't any symbolism, no outright message. It was murder, plain and simple. Sure there were reasons behind it, but she doubted they would be easily explained away by some sort of religious fanaticism.

Rachel found herself trying to slip into the mindset of a criminal profiler. It was a branch of study she'd nearly decided to follow shortly before her training in Quantico. She was decent at it but without the appropriate approach or any strong leads or motivations to consider, she just could not understand the mindset of this killer.

But you know who might…

The thought went through her head as quickly as a lightning strike. And with it came a face she had not considered with any real scrutiny for a few weeks….which was progress, as it had once been a face that had haunted her every single day. It was a stretch and probably a very bad idea but there was also something appealing about the idea that was currently taking shape in her head. There was something dark there, something she was not ready to call out, but she thought there might be something *inside* that darkness worth looking into.

Yeah, and that same person could probably help you with that, too.

She tried to keep the thought away, as well as the face that came with it. But she saw it, peering at her from across a blood-soaked bedroom. A butchered body on the bed and a leering face on the other side, staring at her through thick bifocals. She'd sensed it then, that darkness, and it had never fully left her. It had sat and festered, waiting to come out and to remind her of what the world was capable of.

Thinking of it as she sat at the desk with Jack, she wondered if that darkness had hibernated within her and evolved into something else—maybe a tumor.

You're losing your damned mind, she thought.

Rachel started to stand up from the desk before she was even aware that she'd made the decision. "Jack, do you think you're good here for a few hours?"

"I suppose. Why?"

"I have a hunch…something I'd really rather not take you along on. And something, quite honestly, you'd probably try to talk me out of."

"Sounds promising. Where are you going?"

"I'd rather not say. Just…give me three hours, would you?"

He eyed her suspiciously and said, "Given the erratic behavior you've shown the last few days, please understand that I *have* to ask this: is it concerning this case?"

"Yes," she said. "I want to check on something…"

"Well then, I trust your instincts. I'll look into this Facebook group, try to find some more locals. I might grab a car and head out to the crime scenes again."

"Three hours," she said, already hurrying away from the desk.

"And you're okay?"

No, not at all, she thought.

"Yes," she said. "I'm good."

She turned her back to him and could not stand to look back. She was not only keeping secrets from him, but now she was being deceptive about what she was doing in terms of the case. She supposed she'd have to come clean with him about where she was headed and who she was about to visit before the case came to a close. But she would handle that when the time came. For now, she had to keep convincing *herself* it was a good idea…and that she would not be intimidated when she got there.

***

Rachel had been a special agent for three years when she'd been tasked with bringing in a man that had killed seven people between New Jersey and Virginia. All seven had been killed over a short period of just two weeks and there had been no apparent links to the victims. They knew the murderer's name after the fifth victim due to three fingerprints left behind on the scene; the prints had been etched out in the victim's blood: one on the bedroom door, another on the edge of a kitchen counter, and another on the front doorknob.

He was Alex Lynch, a fifty-three year-old welder with a small trucking company outside of Williamsburg, Virginia. Before he went on his killing spree, he'd never committed a single crime. He was a law-abiding, tax-paying, model American citizen. When Rachel and her partner at the time (and older gentleman that had since been given desk jobs after blowing out a knee on another case) finally caught up to him, he had just taken his seventh victim. The maniac had even applauded Rachel when she found him in the victim's bedroom. Rachel often looked back to that moment, Alex Lynch clapping for her with the victim's blood all over his hands.

Those two weeks of Alex Lynch's life had been studied and documented closely by criminal profilers and ravenous media outlets over the years that followed. According to the official story, Alex Lynch returned a weed eater he had borrowed from a neighbor in his neighborhood along the outskirts of Williamsburg. The men had words over a ding in the weed-eater's cover and in what Lynch later described a "blinding sort of rage where I left my body," he struck his neighbor in the face with the weed eater. He then turned the body of the weed eater around and continued to strike his neighbor's face while he was on the floor. Lynch could not recall when the man died but he kept striking and striking until the entire back end of the weed eater was destroyed, and the lower half of his neighbor's face had been "like jelly."

Lynch later told Rachel and other FBI agents that he'd nearly called the police to report what he'd done, but he'd been too amped up on adrenaline to make any sense of what he'd done. He claimed to have enjoyed what he'd done and within two or three hours had started to figure out how he might be able to do it again without being caught.

His next victim came just fourteen hours later in the small town of Poquoson, in the Hampton Roads area of Virginia. He killed an ex-girlfriend and her husband in their home. The husband was killed with a knife directly through the throat. The ex-girlfriend's fate was considerably worse. When her body was found the following day, she was missing two fingers, most of the skin from her face, and had been stabbed seventeen times. Some of the stab wounds had been done with a knife, but some had been done with a screwdriver.

Lynch then worked his way up to New Jersey, seeming to kill at random. After the neighbor and his ex and her husband, the victims had been total strangers. There had been a man at a rest stop in DC, beheaded and with a collapsed chest cavity courtesy of a brick. Then came the fifth victim, where Lynch had left the prints behind—a model living in Baltimore, twenty-two years old and newly engaged. There had been no sexual assault, no interest in her looks at all, apparently. He'd butchered her, cutting her open from neck to navel as if he had taken a sudden interest in surgery. The sixth victim had been a trucker, sleeping at a 24/7 truck stop; he'd been stabbed twenty times and Rachel and other agents had spent several days trying to figure out if Lynch had bene trying to spell something in the man's torso.

Then there was the seventh victim, an elderly gentleman that Rachel later found she had been just ten minutes away from saving. They'd been able to track Lynch based on security camera footage from the truck stop and that's how Special Agent Rachel Gift had ended up staring Alex Lynch down from across the bed of a recently murdered old man, starting into those eyes pierced with darkness.

And now here she was, revisiting that moment, watching the old man's blood splatter off of Lynch's hands as he applauded her for capturing him.

Nothing good is going to come of this, she told herself as she drove south. *Maybe you truly are losing your mind. Maybe this tumor is messing with your ability to reason.*

For all she knew, maybe it was. But as the interstate unrolled before her, she just dared to hope there were answers to be found. And though the idea of peering past the glasses that covered Alex Lynch's face chilled her, she could not deny that there had been times since his arrest that she wondered if there might indeed be some answers waiting there in that darkness.

CHAPTER TWENTY

The maximum security wing of Arlington County Jail was located on the eleventh floor. Rachel had been inside roughly a dozen prisons for the occasional tasks related to cases, but the one in Arlington was one of the quieter ones she'd ever encountered. The eleventh floor, in particular, was eerily silent; it housed only fourteen men, with the capacity to hold only twenty-six at any given time.

A single guard led Rachel down the eleventh-floor corridor. Unlike the basic cells scattered throughout the ten floors below them, these cells were closed off by solid doors with little slots in them to deliver food, mail, and other necessities. They passed by one door that was opened, revealing a small but tidy interior. Rachel assumed it was the residence of the man she had come to see—a man that was currently waiting for her in the small visiting room at the end of the hallway.

The guard brought her to the end of the hall and gave her a little nod. "I'll be out here if you need me. He's pretty docile most of the time but it's sort of like watching a snake and wondering…you know? He's quiet now, but you just *know* it's going to strike." He seemed to shudder a bit and added, "It's in his eyes, you know?"

Yeah, I know pretty damned well, Rachel thought as the guard escorted her.

Rachel entered the room, and the guard closed the door behind her. Across the room, sitting on a stale-looking couch, was a fifty-three year-old man she had seen far too many times in her lowest moments. Every time she'd gone into a dark room or house looking for clues or suspects, she'd seen him in her mind. She'd seen him clapping with his bloody hands and smiling at her through his glasses.

Currently, Alex Lynch's long black hair hung slightly over his shoulders, tattered and badly in need of combing. The scraggly growth of beard on his chin also needed some attention. He looked at Rachel through thick bifocals and smiled.

"Agent Gift," he said softly. Then, with what appeared to be a genuine smile, he added, "What a *gift* to see you." He sighed, still smiling, and said, "Though, I'm sure you get that joke a lot."

Rachel said nothing. She wasn't even sure what sort of expression was on her face as she sat down in a plastic-covered armchair five feet away from the couch. It had been two and a half years since she'd last seen Alex Lynch…and nearly three since she'd arrested him.

Looking at him now, all she could see was the man she had arrested. Though Alex was cleaned up now (aside from the ratty hair and beard), she still saw him as she'd seen him on the night she'd come in on him shortly after he'd taken his seventh life. There had been a maniacal smile on his face, dried blood under his fingernails, and a gleam in his eyes that had peered out from behind those bifocals—a gleam that seemed to devour her, even when she'd pulled her gun on him and pinned him to the ground. And the bloody clapping, of course.

"I hear you're behaving yourself," Rachel said.

"I'm trying to. I've been reading a lot. Stuff about astrophysics, space, philosophy. Trying to get a grasp on how small I am. How small we *all* are."

The maniacal gleam was not in his eyes. All Rachel could take from his current state was curiosity. She knew what she wanted to ask him but also knew that she was opening up a Pandora's box of trauma and horror by being here.

"Something's troubling you?" Alex said. "Are you still having the nightmares?"

"No," she snapped.

He was referring to the two visits she'd made to him in the six months following his arrest. She'd had nightmares about him. There had been two different ones; in one, she had been the model victim in Baltimore, her chest and stomach split open. She had seen her entire murder in dream-form. The grotesque nature of her own murder had been far too vibrant and kept her from getting a sound night's sleep for nearly a month. The second dream, she'd seen the murders through Alex Lynch's eyes and had even felt the joy of the act as he'd slit the victims open.

She hated that she'd even told him about the nightmares. But she knew that with men like Lynch, the more power they felt they had, the more willing they were to play ball. And honestly, if Rachel was being honest with herself, it had been almost therapeutic to tell Alex Lynch about the nightmares She wasn't sure why, but it was the sad reality of the situation.

Rachel did not want to give him any further opportunities to speculate, so she pushed out the reason for her visit. "I need to know why you did it," she said. "I need to know what it was about your life or your mindset at the time that pushed you to it. All of the court documents and psychiatric referrals state that you appeared to be of a sound mind at the time you were questioned and the way you describe each of the murders suggests you were also of a sound mind when you killed them—something you yourself have admitted to."

"Ahh," Alex said. He stared at her for a moment and then to his hands, which were folded in his lap. "You may not want to hear this, but I don't identify with the man that killed those seven people. I am not naïve enough to think that I was someone else when I did it, but when I try to recall what was going through my head, it makes no sense to me."

"But do you remember what you were feeling at the time?" Rachel asked. "We have reams and reams of studies and research that sow the vast difference in the mindset of someone that only kills once and someone that kills multiple people. There's an enormous difference, particularly when it comes to those that were not muddied with pleas of insanity."

"Well, naturally," Alex said. "The first time, it's new and exciting and you get lost in it. It's much like losing your virginity. There is much nervousness and slight panic the first time. But then when it's over and the delight has been had...you start to plan for the second time. What can you do different? What did you enjoy and want to keep the same? And then by the third or fourth time, it starts to feel quite natural."

The explanation unnerved her, but she pressed on. She knew she could not spend more than half an hour or so here. She fully intended to be back in Baltimore in the three hours she'd promised.

"How many did you kill before you stopped having any hang-ups on the right-and-wrong of it?" she asked.

"The second one. During that one...even if I *had* cared, it would not have been enough to make me stop."

Rachel cringed when she thought of the second and third victims. The ex and her husband. She saw the ex, the screwdriver sticking out of her pelvis. He'd then cut a vertical line down her man's navel and partially disemboweled him. It had been one of the grislier scenes, but not the worst. That had been the seventh victim, the elderly man whom Alex had killed by stabbing him in the heart with a pair of scissors and then removing several patches of skin and tissue with the same scissors. The scissors had been found shoved down the poor man's throat. It was the only time in Rachel's career that she feared she might throw up at a murder scene. There were still times when she saw a simple pair of scissors and felt her stomach clench up.

"You need help," Alex said, picking up on her hesitation. "Is that what it is? You are after a killer that is hard to pin down so you are here to ask me my opinions. You want to know why we kill. Something like that?"

"Not quite as simple as that, but sure" she agreed. "We have a man killing women that are signed up for fertility treatments. It's a solid link but we still can't locate the man. We're hoping that if we can figure out *why* he's doing it, it might lead us to him a bit faster. The way in which he is killing sort of lines up with some of what you did...to the trucker in particular."

"Twenty times," he said with a smirk. "And no...I was not trying to spell out anything."

Rachel glared at him, letting him know that she was not here just to hear him gloat about his murders.

"How many has he killed so far?" Alex asked. He leaned forward with great interest, peering at her through those thick glasses.

"Three. And they are happening quickly. He's not taking much time between his victims." She was aware that she really should not be giving him these sorts of details. But when it was all boiled down, she should not be here at all. She figured if she had crossed the line into this bizarre territory, she may as well go for broke.

"How is he killing them?"

"With a knife," Rachel said. "The attacks are vicious...not just one stab wound, but several. And they seem to be made in a hectic and angry fashion. There's nothing slow and methodical about it."

"I would assume, then, that the killer has nothing personal against the women. He is acting out only because of something they are doing that he disagrees with. More than that, the way he's doing it leads me to think that he hates these women. He *loathes* them. He's doing it quickly with a knife rather than taking his time with it because he can't stand being around them. He wants it done quickly so he can not only get away from the scene, but so he can be done with that woman." He stopped here, as if considering his own comment, and added, "I would assume it is not the fact that they are undergoing the treatments that is causing him to select these women."

"It seems fairly apparent that's *exactly* what he's doing."

Alex smiled and shook his head. "You misunderstand me. Yes, I believe the killer may be headhunting these women through clinics or services. That makes sense. But the way they are dispatching their victims...it's odd, given the situation. It makes me think they are killing not for their own needs or beliefs. These sorts of killings, so violent from what you describe, sound like either control or jealousy issues. Or both."

She was beginning to get irritated because it seemed like he was intentionally speaking in riddles. Maybe he was trying to get as much enjoyment out of this visit as possible because no one ever came to visit him.

"I'm not quite following you," she said, hating to admit it.

"What I'm trying to say is that the killer is likely not killing these women simply because they have made appointments for these fertility treatments. It seems to me—and I could be wrong, granted—that the killer is going after these women because the treatments will *give them* the chance to conceive. Meaning, perhaps…"

"That the killer has not been able to have children."

Alex gave her a little mocking clap and nodded. "Ah, there you go."

She eyed him with confusion, not sure what to think of him. He said he had changed and the past fifteen minutes backed that up. Yet, at the same time, she had seen the grisly murders this man committed. It was as if a demon had been yanked out of him and replaced with someone capable of sincerity and reason.

"Did any of this help?" Alex asked.

"You know, I think it did." She got to her feet and the words *"Thank you"* were on her lips. But then her mind brought forth images of his victims: a man disemboweled, a woman with most of her skin removed from her face and chest, the man with scissors jammed down his throat, a man with a hatchet buried in his crotch…

"Guard," she said, her voice a bit shaky.

"Leaving already?" Alex said from behind her. And there was a bit too much cheer in his voice for Rachel's liking.

"Yes. I'm done here."

"That's a shame. There's something different about you now. I can't quite place it, but…you're struggling with something other than this case, aren't you?" He chuckled and added, "You can tell me what it is if you want."

Rachel thought of Lynch's ex-girlfriend and the model, all torn right open. She felt like that as she stood in front of him—like he'd ripped her open and could see every single thing about her, even her secrets. And despite that, she felt a question crawling across her tongue. It was unexpected and certainly not one she would have ever dreamed of asking him. But being here in front of him, things were different and she could not help herself. As she asked the question, she could almost sense the tumor in her brain pushing it out for her.

"What's it like? Being that close to...to death?"

He wasted no time with his answer. It seemed as if he'd spent some time contemplating it himself over the years. "Intimate, but in a very polarizing way. For me, it's being right there on the edge of it...knowing that one day I, too, will be on that edge, looking out the other way. But to give someone else that push...it's like nothing you can imagine."

For a split second, she almost wanted to know what he was talking about. With the tumor, she was definitely worried about her own mortality and was more aware of it than she ever had been before. Before she could say anything else, Rachel finally turned away for good and headed for the door.

"That must be what I see that's different about you," he said. She never turned around but did pause by the door, her hand frozen as she reached for the knob.

"Something's messed up with you," he said, almost insightfully. "Something's...*broken.*"

She said nothing. She knocked quickly on the door and waited for the guard to respond. When he did, Rachel slipped right out and the guard closed the door behind her. It felt like she'd stepped out of an icebox and into the comforting heat of a woodside fire on a winter's day.

"You okay?" the guard asked.

"Yes, I'm fine."

Though, if she were being honest, she almost felt as if the eyes of Alex Lynch were somehow still on her, even through the closed door. She exited the jail as quickly as she could without seeming out of sorts. When she returned to her car, she sat there for a moment, quiet and unmoving. She stared at the building, going over everything Alex had said.

Something's...broken.

He'd meant it about her, but she wondered if maybe there was something more there. Could it be the reason someone simply snapped and started killing people? Or could the brokenness be a more tangible thing, a brokenness that served as motivation—as motive?

With that idea turning over and over in her head like a rough stone being polished, Rachel started the car and headed back to Baltimore. She was leaving with no real leads, but with a personal awakening she was not quite ready to face and an idea that might help them pry this case open just a little farther.

CHAPTER TWENTY ONE

Sitting down with a glass of wine, she grabbed her phone off of the coffee table. Her hands were trembling a bit as she swiped up to unlock it. She was not nervous, but anxious. It was not too dissimilar from the feeling she'd once experienced in college when she'd been sleeping with her roommate's boyfriend. The thrill of sneaking around, of knowing it what she was about to do was *wrong.* Back then, the anticipation and build-up of meeting with him was often more satisfying than the act itself.

That was, of course, after she'd been gang raped and beaten ten minutes after leaving a bar. Sleeping with her roommate's boyfriend had been another mistake in the chain of bad decisions that followed.

But that was not the case now—the anticipation was not quite as good as the final act. No, what she planned to do—and had been doing for a little over a week now—was *much more* satisfying than the build-up. She still felt new to it…like she had no idea what she was doing. Then again, taking a life was taking a life. There were lots of ways to do it, she supposed, but the end result was the same: another death dealt out into the world.

She opened up Facebook and typed out the same search in the search bar that she'd been using for the past month or so: *Family Focus Fertility.* The page came up and she clicked on it…but something was different. Something had changed. She stared at the screen for a moment, a flood of rage storming her heart.

The screen was white and grey, with a simple message in the center: *This is a private group.*

She took a sip of her wine, hoping it would battle the anger that was rising up in her. She could feel it consuming every nerve and muscle and before she knew what she was doing, she threw the wine glass across the room. It exploded against the wall, red wine splattering the wall like blood spray.

Oddly enough, she briefly thought of her students. What would they say if they saw her reacting in such a way. Such rage…such hatred.

Well, they'd likely frown upon me killing people, too, she thought. It was a thought that brought a dry, breathy laughter up out of her throat.

She went back to her phone and picked it up, doing her best to settle herself.

Yesterday, the page had been public. And all the days before that when she had gone on to hunt for victims, it had also been set to public. So why the hell was it private now?

Because they're on to you, she thought. *You knew at some point, the police were going to not only get involved, but probably even figure out how you were doing it. Now is that time. They've figured out how you found those women and have contacted the page administrators.*

Having known something like this would probably happen did not make it any easier to accept. She'd had a simple way to find her victims right in the palm of her hand—easy access, as if it were meant to be. And now that was gone. Now, if she wanted to continue her work, she was going to have to find some other way to do it.

She tossed her phone down on the couch and walked over to where the glass had shattered all along the floor. Red wine dripped down the wall and created a puddle on her carpet. She knew how much trouble it would be to get that red wine stain out of the carpet, but she could figure that out later. Because even as she started picking up the portions and shards of glass from the floor, her mind was already moving forward.

While her easy hunting grounds had indeed been taken away from her, she still had one more visit to make. She had already picked her next target. She had a name, an address, and a pretty good idea of when the treatment date had been scheduled. She would attend to that business first. There was no sense in ruining that moment with worries about where she would find others to go after.

She was so distracted by these thoughts that she sliced right into her thumb as she was picking up a bigger sliver of glass. With a hiss of pain, she pulled her hand away. She looked to her thumb and smiled as she watched the little trickle of blood run down it. She sat there on the floor and watched the blood slowly run down her hand, transfixed by it and just as eager as ever to get on with her work.

The Facebook group being Private was not a big deal, but it still had her spooked. She knew she was not ready to strike right now. But she could still get out there and make sure the details of her next victim were unchanged. She had to be precise in all that she did, and sometimes that meant putting in some extra work. Besides…it wasn't like that was the only Facebook Page for people having fertility issues. There had to be hundreds of them, and at least a few within areas close by—DC, Alexandria, maybe Pittsburg.

She went to the bathroom and washed the blood from her hand. The cut was shallow and she was able to easily cover it with some Neosporin and a Band Aid. With that done, she headed outside and got into her car. As usual, she felt as if some other person slid in behind the controls of her mind as she guided the car to the residence of her next victim. The night seemed thick, like sludge as she drove through it. Like always, the world felt a little different when she headed out with murder on her mind. Even if it was not the night she would be committing the act, it was as if the darkness *knew*.

It wasn't a very long drive to the next victim's house. The drive there was like a blur, as if she'd been teleported. She was aware of the road, the lines, the headlights that passed by her, but she wasn't really there at all. She could have easily been somewhere else, maybe even back at the school, waiting for her children to arrive. There was something pleasant about such a feeling of detachment. It meant she could be somewhere else, some other place where she'd never killed, where she'd never been raped and left without the ability to give birth to a child.

Somehow, through her darkened haze, she arrived. She pulled in front of the house, in a small suburb. She parked on the side of the road opposite the house, not wanting to seem too obvious. She'd parked in this same spot multiple times as she staked out her victim—the same way she'd staked out all of the others.

It was after six, so the husband was not home. And because they had no kids, her victim was all by herself.

I could do it now...I could do it tonight.

It was tempting, but she was not in the right mind space. Plus, she'd left her knife at home. She'd come to understand that she did not mind the act of killing, but she couldn't just do it at any time. She had given herself a timeline and dates to adhere to; she felt that straying from that in any way would be a recipe for disaster.

She sat in front of that unremarkable house in a flat, featureless suburb until she watched the last light go off. Without looking at her phone or the clock on the dashboard, she knew it would be somewhere between 10:40 and 11:00. When she did check the time, she smiled. It was 10:52.

Just like clockwork.

The confirmation of how well she knew the victim's schedule was enough to remove the frustration of having the Facebook page taken away from her. Now, with this bit of confidence, she almost found it amusing.

They thought they'd stopped her, but she had at least one more surprise for them.

CHAPTER TWENTY TWO

Rachel was expecting the third-degree from Jack when she returned to the station. She was back roughly half an hour earlier than she'd projected, and she found Jack still sitting at the desk in the back of the building. He was now on a laptop and when Rachel looked over his shoulder, she saw that he had accessed the station's records directory.

"What are you looking for?" she asked. Her hope was that by starting the conversation on her terms about something he was doing, any questions about what she'd been up to would be temporarily set aside—or maybe even not asked at all.

"I could only find four more women in that Facebook group from Baltimore or any surrounding areas," he said. "One of them had not posted in about six months, but that's because she died in a car accident on the Beltway. She and her husband, both dead. Another seems to have moved several months ago, now residing on Orlando, Florida. I'm checking for any dings on her record right now and so far have found none. As for the other two, they have completely spotless records. Nothing to go off of at all."

"So nothing, then…"

"Well, nothing *new*. I did place a call to the bureau and had someone of the task force get in touch with the group's moderators. As of about an hour ago, it's been set to Private. So unless the killer is actually part of the group—which, let's be honest, would be a stupid move on their part—his hunting grounds are now closed."

"That's good news," she said. She sat on the edge of the desk, as there was only one chair. She was fully expecting him to ask her where she'd gone but it never came. She'd likely tell him before all was said and done but for now she was still trying to convince herself it had been a smart move. Visiting Alex Lynch had opened her eyes to some new insights and theories but some core part of her still felt cold and dirty for seeking him out for advice. The silence between them felt thick and she figured she may as well mention what she suspected before Jack could comment on the trip she'd just taken.

"Since you're already on the network," she said, "I'd like to pursue another avenue. I'd like to cross-reference the records of both clinics in the hope of finding someone that underwent fertility treatments at both Regency and Greenfield Women's Health Services."

"Why would they undergo treatments at *both?*" he asked. But the nodding of his head at the end of the question showed that he already knew the answer before the question had been fully formed.

Rachel went ahead and answered for him anyway. "Because the treatments could have failed. What if your killer had tried treatments at both clinics and came away with none of them working? What if these are revenge killings?"

"You mean wanting to take that chance away from other women?" Jack asked.

"Maybe."

Jack nodded, leaning back in the seat and rubbing at his eyes. "So, you think the killer is a woman?"

"I'm not sure what I think," she said. "I just think it's one possibility that could be explored."

"Okay," Jack said, starting to look through some of the files and gathered forms they'd collected during the course of the case. So…how far back are we talking? Maybe a full year or so?"

"At least," Rachel said, also starting to dig through the papers. "If we can find women that attended *both* clinics and had no luck at either place, it shouldn't be too long of a list. We can check those names against police records and that might give us something to work with."

It only took her a few moments to realize that they did not yet have the information she needed. She got on the phone with Regency as Jack called up Greenfield Women's Health Services and just like that, it felt like there was a spark of hope to propel them along.

"Regency Fertility Clinic," a cheerful female voice answered. "How can I help you?"

"This is Special Agent Rachel Gift," she said, wondering if this was one of the several women she'd spoken to since arriving in town on the case. "I need a list of names of patients that have come in for treatments over the last year but had no success."

"Well, I can't exactly and that sort of thing out, ma'am."

Ah, so it's not *someone I've already spoken to,* Rachel thought. "Could you please connect me with Dr. Jergens, please?"

There was a heavy hesitation from the other end, followed by a resigned "Please hold."

Apparently, Jack was having no such problems. He was speaking cordially into the phone, giving someone an email address to send the list to. When he hung up the phone, he gave Rachel a playfully taunting sort of look.

After about a minute and a half, another female voice sounded out in Rachel's ear. "Agent Gift," said Dr. Jergens. "What can I do for you this time?"

"As I told the receptionist, we're now looking for a list of unsuccessful treatments. Anyone that has come in over the last year or so for treatments and had no success at all."

"And I believe what my receptionist told you was absolutely accurate. We can't just give out names like that. This is highly personal information, Agent Gift."

"I appreciate and respect that. And I also understand the position I am putting you in. But I can tell you with one hundred percent confidence that if we don't get this list, I'll be calling you in about a day or two to ask for information on yet another dead woman."

The silence that met this comment sounded like victory to Rachel. She honestly did not like to be so direct and forward when it came to this sort of personal information, but she did not see that she had any other choice, given the circumstances.

"You're right," Jergens said, though it was abundantly clear that she was not happy to admit such a thing. "I'll get a list together and send it over within the hour. But I'll also be sending a form for you to sign indicating that you'll do nothing outside of this case with the information."

"Of course. Thank you, Dr. Jergens."

She ended the call with a restless hope in her heart. She felt that this hunch was a strong one and there would, at the very least, be answers to be found there. She did her best to keep looking through Facebook groups and the existing paperwork as they waited for Jergens's email.

It came twenty-two minutes later, and Jack printed it off right away. The list was much shorter than Rachel had expected; it consisted of just a single sheet of paper with thirty-nine names. Jack also handed Rachel the other form Jergens had mentioned. She signed it without really even looking at it, her eyes and full attention already on the list of thirty-nine women Jergens had sent over.

"How many names on the Greenfield list?" she asked Jack.

"Twenty-six. And according to the administrative assistant I spoke with, she said she did not think the chances of a woman going to two different clinics would be very high. The sheer cost of it alone would be a significant deterrent, even with insurance kicking in."

Rachel scanned Regency's list, quickly eyeing each of the thirty-nine names. "Okay, so let's compare," she said. "Your list is shorter, so you read the names off to me."

He did, starting with a woman named Alyssa Cole—who was not on Rachel's list. It was tedious work, like some sort of odd word puzzle, but it paid off when Jack read off the eleventh name.

"Next, we have Gemma Chapman."

Rachel read down the list, quite sure she'd seen the name while eliminating others. Sure enough, she was right there, four names from the bottom. Her treatment with Regency had occurred nine months ago.

"She's right here," Rachel said. She stood to her feet, tapping excitedly at the name on her list. "Her treatment came back as negative a little over nine months ago. You?"

"Three months ago at Greenfield."

Rachel pulled up the station network, navigated to the criminal database, and typed in *Gemma Chapman*. Jack filed in behind her, watching the screen load over her shoulder. Rachel could feel a collective surge of adrenaline between the two of them as the possibility of a strong lead began to spring up in front of them.

"Well I'll be damned," Jack said from over her shoulder.

Rachel read the details of the page out loud, a habit she had never been able to break herself out of. "DUI four years ago but most recently, she did a very brief stint of jailtime for assault against a woman in a public park a little over a year ago. The other woman required stitches and pressed charges."

"Seems like someone filled with aggression to me," Jack said. "Throw in failed fertility treatments from two different clinics…yeah, I think that might be a pretty good fit."

"Same," Rachel said, clicking on the tab for personal info. She plugged Gemma Chapman's current address into her phone and got to her feet. "So, let's go pay Miss Chapman a visit."

***

Gemma Chapman lived in a modest home in a blue-collar neighborhood. A tilted plastic flamingo sat all alone just in front of an entirely dead flowerbed. A few hanging ferns gave the porch a bit of color but other than that, the house was unremarkable. The porch showed signs of disrepair—paint flaking from the posts, a single spot where termites had feasted at some point in the past.

Rachel took the lead and knocked on the door. As she waited to see if there was anyone home, she was answered in the form of a television at low volume. Shuffling footsteps could be heard a few moments later and then the door was opened just a crack.

"Who's there?" a woman said, revealing only one eye and a long, angular nose.

"I'm Special Agent Rachel Gift, and I'm accompanied by my partner, Jack Rivers. We were hoping to ask you a few questions."

"Me?" she asked, sounding genuinely confused.

"Yes, ma'am."

The woman, presumably Gemma Chapman, opened the door the remainder of the way. "Can I ask what this is about?" she asked. She was dressed in a ratty tee shirt and a pair of sweatpants. She was slightly overweight, most of it showing in her face. Her brown hair looked as if it had not been washed in about a week. And though Rachel hated to think such a thing about anyone right off the bat, the woman just looked straight-out sad.

"You're Gemma Chapman, correct?" Rachel asked.

"I am. Please...come on in and have a seat."

She gestured to the couch and armchair in her small living room. A TV was mounted on the wall, currently tuned to the Weather Channel. Rachel sat down, always aware that it was best to look at ease and non-threatening when getting information out of people.

"Mrs. Chapman, we are currently investigating a series of murders that seems to be targeting women that are scheduled for fertility treatments."

Gemma nodded, as if she understood perfectly. "I saw something about those killings on the news this morning. It's terrible."

Rachel watched the woman's face, trying to get a proper gauge on her reaction to why they were here. She knew Jack would be too, and that he was typically very good at reading the immediate reaction of people that have just received any sort of jarring news. From what Rachel could tell, Gemma Chapman did not seem scared that they were here; confusion remained, genuine and unmoving, from her face.

"Well, we're visiting you because we're doing cross checks of women that have done business with both clinics," Rachel said. "And as you might imagine, your criminal history gave us a bit of concern."

"Mrs. Chapman, do you mind walking us through what happened about a year or so ago out in that public park?"

She nodded and the curiosity on her face was replaced by sadness. "I was angry, sad...and very dumb," she said. "A few years back, my husband and I divorced. He badly wanted kids and I was unable to have them. But we did some tests and found that there were fertility treatments I could take. He didn't like the idea. He had this macho idea that those treatments were cheating. He decided that if couldn't have kids the old-fashioned way, he didn't want them. So, it led to lots of arguments and an eventual divorce. But the idea just stayed in my head and I decided that even without him around, I wanted to try. I'd get a kid and manage to have it and raise it without him.

"I met with doctors and they all told me the chances were slim. But I set up an appointment anyway."

"With Regency first, correct?" Rachel asked.

"Yes. Now, of course, my little incident in the park occurred a bit before I first tried the treatments. There was this fundraiser for Mary's House—this sort of recue home for young mothers with nowhere to go. I went by to show my support, maybe even make a donation. And when I was there, I saw that there was a booth for one of the local pregnancy centers. There were these two women there, talking about their recent pregnancies and it just…I lost it. Looking back on it now, I know it was absolutely foolish of me to even *be* there. I knew it would depress me, sort of be a trigger So yes…the woman I attacked was talking about how she delivered twins and their laughing…it got to me. I acted irrationally, and I have regretted it every day since."

When she stopped talking, she took a deep breath in and when she let it out, a trail of tears came spilling out of both eyes. They came seemingly out of nowhere, taking Rachel slightly by surprise. They came with such suddenness that Rachel was inclined to believe they might be genuine.

"When was the last time you visited either of the clinics?" Jack asked.

"It's been about three months ago, I suppose. It was at Greenfield…sort of a check-up." She eyed them both and the reality of why they were here slowly dawned on her. There was fury there, but a deep sadness as well. "I guess you're here to see if I'm the killer, is that it? The crazy bitch that can't have a baby…the one that attacked that perfectly nice and happy woman at the park. Sorry to disappoint you but, no…I'm not a killer. And it's fucking insulting to think you'd even come here to suggest it."

Rachel and Jack both sat in stunned silence for a moment. Gemma had not quite exploded on them, but it had been close. And it had seemed to come out of nowhere, making Rachel wonder just how deeply wounded she was over her failed marriage and the inability to have a child. How long had she been holding on to it...and did she blame herself for her infertility?

"Can you provide proof of your whereabouts for the nights over the last week or so?" Rachel asked.

"I'm not sure how to prove I've been sitting here at home," she said. "Because that's all I've done. It's all I've done since I got back home from my little three-day stint in prison. Sitting at home, not wanting to go outside. Only going out when I need groceries, or to work, or...it's been miserable."

Rachel wasn't sure if the woman was trying to make them feel sorry for her or if it was just starting to come naturally for her. Whichever it was, Rachel could not deny that she was truly starting to feel bad for coming her to question her. Sure, she had beaten a new mother rather badly in a public park, but there were clearly scars of self-rejection and loathing holding the poor woman down.

"We can prove it if there is any traceable internet activity," Jack said. "Though, to be honest, these killings we are looking into took place late at night. So if you aren't a night owl..." He shrugged, apparently starting to feel just as bad as Rachel about being here.

"Well, I guess I'm in luck," Gemma said. "I'm not sleeping much these days, and when I do it's usually a nap on the couch mid-day. I have a pretty bad habit of Amazon-shopping far too late into the night." Then an *a-ha* sort of look came over her face. "Oh, and four nights ago, I was out of town...in Bethesda, visiting my mom. I stayed over and we had breakfast together before I left. So maybe that will help, too."

She didn't say these things in an angry or condescending tone. To Rachel, it seemed as if the woman truly wanted to help. "Would you be willing to provide your computer and your mother's address?" Rachel asked.

Rachel saw Gemma struggling to keep her anger down, trying her best to keep from having a legitimate outburst. "I regret what I did," she said, speaking slowly and looking to both of them with an intense stare, "But I don't deserve this. I had nothing to do with these murders and it's things like this that make me think I'll never outlive what I did. It'll always come back and back and back." With each *back,* she stomped hard on the floor.

"I apologize for that," Rachel said. "But if you'd just—"

"Yes, you can have the damn laptop. My phone, my laptop...anything else you need. Car, house...you need a blood sample?"

Something in this almost brazen way of granting their request told Rachel that Gemma Chapman was very likely not their killer. That, plus what she'd said about online shopping and the visit to her mother, added up to yet another strike for her and Jack. She was so certain of Gemma's innocence that even as Jack took down the number of Gemma's grandmother, Rachel was already rummaging through her mind, trying to figure out what their next move would be.

And much to her dismay, she was not coming up with much.

As she and Jack headed to the door, leaving a frustrated Gemma Chapman scowling in her living room, Rachel felt her phone buzzing in her pocket. She was somehow certain it would be Dr. Greene with more bad news for her. Maybe he had been wrong and had given her too much time to look forward to. Maybe she really only had a few months left, maybe even less.

But when she checked it, she saw that it was Paige's babysitter, Becka, FaceTiming her. A flash of worry sped through her. "I have to take this," she told Jack as she hurried through the front door and onto Gemma's porch.

"Hello?" she said, answering on the third ring.

The face that appeared was not Becka's but Paige's. As usual, she was smiling. The kid was used to the often hectic schedule of her parents so a few days away from her mother wasn't going to bring her down. And even though Rachel felt a bit let down from the way things with Gemma had gone, she found that she was happy to hear from Paige.

"Hey, Mommy. You busy? Can we talk?"

Before Rachel could answer, she heard Becka calling out from off-screen. "I'm so sorry, Mrs. Gift! I told her to wait until later!"

"It's okay, Becka. So…what's up kiddo?"

"We got a handout at school today for soccer try-outs," Paige said. "It's next Saturday, and I really want to go."

Jack passed by, leaving the porch and heading down to the car to give Rachel some privacy. He grinned at her, as he always did when he knew she was on the phone with Paige. Typically, speaking to her daughter cheered her up considerably when they were on the road.

"Well, go ahead and put it on the calendar." What she did not say was that she'd not once ever heard Paige mention being interested in soccer. But she knew that Paige was in a very experimental phase right now. She wanted to try everything, and Rachel and Peter supported it.

"Will you be back in time?" Paige asked.

"Before next Saturday? Absolutely. Honey, I'm hoping to be back home in another couple of days."

"Oh, okay."

"Everything else good?"

"Yeah! Becka is making pancakes for dinner. And then Daddy is going to take me out for ice cream."

"That's whole lot of sugar. Make sure you brush your teeth really good before bed."

"I will. Bye, Mommy!"

It had been a brief conversation but, as was always the case when Paige called, it felt as if she's been tossed into a whirlwind and spit out. Even in little conversations, her daughter was a little force of nature. As Rachel slowly placed the phone back into her pocket, she realized that she missed Paige more than she usually did when she was on a trip.

It's because you're keeping a secret from her, she thought. *Really, you're lying by omission.*

This was true and she knew she'd have to deal with it eventually. She slowly made her way down Gemma Chapman's porch steps, suddenly feeling guilty for leaving Paige in the dark. She was likely too young to fully understand what her diagnosis meant but, still...she deserved to know. So did Peter, and so did Jack.

The guilt ate at her for just a moment, but she then shoved it away. For now, she had to focus on this case. This case was an island off the coast of every other part of her life and she could not leave it until they had their killer.

And with no real leads to speak of, she figured they only had the papers and records back at the station. Maybe they'd missed some obvious connection buried in the mundane nature of lists of people's names and medical records. There had to be something there. And once they found it, they could get their killer...and she could *then* devote her time and energy to figuring out how to break the news to her family.

But first...the case. She held that list of priorities firm in her mind as she got back into the car and, without a word, started the engine and left Gemma Chapman's house.

CHAPTER TWENTY THREE

Back at the station, she sat at the desk and scanned through all of the files and papers again. As she did, she found herself on the verge of getting sidetracked. She still had her big secret—her tumor diagnosis that still sat heavy on her shoulder like a parrot that would not shut up. The guilt she'd felt at Gemma's house tried to keep coming back, fueled by the sight of Paige's face during the FaceTime call. And even when she was able to look beyond that guilt, there was the memory of what had happened to her while chasing down Maria Oliver. More accurately, she was reminded of how she'd been shown yet another glimpse of the mortality she was going to have to get a handle on.

Hey, her body said. *You're not the invincible, star agent you've always been. There's a tumor in your head, remember? What the hell are you trying to prove?*

She also found herself thinking of Peter and Paige, back at home with no clue at all that she had essentially been handed her death warrant. She could sense the all-consuming guilt behind that little nugget, but she pushed it aside for now. She figured she could process through it when the case was finished. Because the longer her mind spent away from the facts and twists of this case, the more time the killer had to target his (or, as she was currently thinking, *her*) next victim.

With no further leads or hope of answers, they had no real path forward other than once again scouring the records, paperwork, and patient lists. Combining that with what they now knew of the Facebook group, she felt there *had* to be some sort of answer buried in it all.

While Rachel poured through the print outs, patient lists, and station network, Jack was online, searching for other fertility support groups—not just online, but local meet-and-greet type meetings. Every now and then, he would scribble down a name on a nearby pad and then continue his search.

"There's at least three in the city," he said, looking up from his scribbled notes. "But from what I can find, none of them really see all that much activity. Also, because it's a public forum of sorts, it's going to be tough to get names."

"I think that's okay, though," Rachel said. "Our killer would have to be very stupid to go looking for victims at a public meeting."

Jack nodded, but he kept looking. Rachel understood the mindset, though; sometimes there was gold buried in the most unlikely of places. Also, when there were no solid leads, this was the only real avenue they had to take.

Again and again, Rachel found herself distracted by her own running inner-monologue. She could not help but wonder if it would be less distracting if she just told someone. Yes, Jack was the more sensible choice because he was *right there* but she was still struck by the feeling that Peter needed to be the first to know.

"Jesus," she murmured as she tossed down the file she had currently bene looking through. The papers, the files, the laptops, Jack…suddenly, her world felt far too hectic and crowded.

"You okay?" Jack asked, peering up from the laptop screen.

"Yeah, just flustered."

"You're not going to abandoned me for another three-hour excursion, are you?" he joked.

"No. Just…just going to go to the restroom."

Hey, look, another lie, she told herself. Or maybe it was some disembodied voice on her head—hell, maybe it was the voice of the tumor, calling her out.

Still mostly unfamiliar with the station, Rachel did indeed head for the restrooms but passed by them. She wandered around the back of the station and came to two conferences rooms. One was a bit larger and was slightly messy, an indication that it had been used at some point during the day. But at the end of the hall, she found a smaller one. It looked as if it had not been used any time recently. When she walked in and closed the door behind her, she noticed the smell of stale whiteboard cleaner spray and the ghost of a lingering coffee smell. With the room in total darkness, Rachel found her way to the corner and sat down.

She closed her eyes, letting the peacefulness of her makeshift isolation chamber sink into her. Her parading thoughts slowed down, allowing her to better prioritize them. In the dark, she could temporarily shove aside all matters pertaining to the tumor and her secrecy of it. She could now better focus on the case, trying to find some straight and narrow thread she and Jack had not yet been able to unravel.

She re-examined each crime scene in her mind. She went back through every conversation she'd had with people that had all eventually ended in dead-ends. Standing out above them all was her brief meeting with Alex Lynch. While it was a bit creepy to think of his deadened stare in the darkness of the conference room, she made herself go back there. Rachel did her best to replay the entire conversation. And though she could not remember it all, the highlights were very easy to recall.

Why would the killer want these women dead?

It was the core of the entire case. They thought they'd stumbled across the reasoning a few times but it had never quite panned out. Even the way they'd found Gemma Chapman had seemed promising at first—and there was still something to that reasoning that stood out to Rachel. Maye there was something there. And if it was…then maybe it would be advantageous to stop looking it the entire ordeal through the eyes of a killer. Maybe it would make more sense to look at it through the eyes of someone that wanted to be a mother but couldn't.

Alex had said it perfectly: *the killer is going after these women because the treatments will give them the chance to conceive.*

Rachel thought of how she might have felt if she had been trying to get pregnant but everyone around her seemed to be having no problems. While it was a sad scenario, she felt like there had to be more to it. What if the killer already knew what it was like to be a mother and something about the treatments was triggering her? If that *were* the case, what could possibly happen to make a woman snap so badly that she would go after women trying everything they could to have a baby. How could…

Slowly, Rachel got to her feet. Could it be that simple? Had they been looking at this thing through the wrong lens the entire time?

Maybe it wasn't *just* about the killer losing their chance. Maybe they had no chance to conceive at all.

It was an interesting thought, but there had to be something more to it. There had to be some catalyst that spurred it on. Rachel then started to wonder what would be the one thing that might drive a mother to absolute madness…?

She rushed for the conference room door and left the darkness behind. She did not run back to the desk where Jack was still at work, but she moved much faster than she normally would while inside. When she approached the desk at something of a trot, Jack looked up to her, perplexed.

"I know you're getting tired of hearing this question," he said, "but…are you okay?"

"Listen…I think we're on the right track," Rachel said. "But I don't think we've pushed the line enough What if the killer—assuming it's a

105

woman—did once have her chance but now it's gone. What if the killer once had a child but the child died and now, for whatever reason, she can't have more?"

The skepticism on his face was brief, almost instantly overruled by excitement and clarity. "Damn, that does make a lot of sense." Nodding, he looked back to the laptop and to the files and papers spread all around their desk. "Looks like we need to start looking for something a bit more specific, huh?"

"Looks that way," she said, already starting to sift through the paperwork again.

***

The day was coming to a close and at some point, during their renewed and refreshed search, Rachel had somehow managed to drink three cups of coffee. She felt it in her nerves, making her slightly jittery. They'd been at it for about an hour and a half, working so feverishly through the papers and on the phone that Rachel almost felt as if they had some weird-part time job at a call center.

She was looking back through the limited criminal records of the staff from both clinics when Jack spoke up, his voice somewhere between doubtful and hopeful. "Hey, Rachel...do you have the copy of the full employee list from Regency?"

"Yeah," she said, thumbing through the papers and finding it. She slid the list over to him, trying to latch on to the tone of hope she'd heard in his voice. "Do you think you might have something?"

"Maybe," he said, placing the list next to another sheet of paper. He eyed them back and forth, his eyes bouncing as if he were watching a tennis match. Slowly, he started to nod and his eyes grew just a bit brighter.

"What is it?" Rachel asked.

"There's a doctor currently employed by Regency Fertility Clinic named Pauline Vick. She's been working for Regency for seven years, but she's also on the consult list for Greenfield. Not sure how long she's being doing it, but there she is, on both lists."

It sounded like such a stupid thing to overlook, but then again they had been so focused on the doctors and patients that the consultants working out of Greenfield had never even crossed their radar. Regency did not work with consultants, only with other high-end doctors from larger hospitals, so they'd not had lists to compare.

"Is it really that simple?" she said. "How did we miss it?"

"Well, the Greenfield consult list isn't very long and there are *none* for Regency," Jack said. "No one has come out and said it, but I get the feeling Greenfield is considered almost second-rate to Regency. It seems that a lot of Greenfield's doctors—and even some of their nurses—sort of freelance in and out to local doctor's offices and hospitals."

"I'll run a Google search if you'll check the database," Rachel said.

Jack answered in the way of instantly turning back to the laptop and typing the name into the database. Having just the one computer, Rachel took her phone from her pocket and typed the name Pauline Vick into the search bar. She was honestly not expecting much more than a Facebook profile, or maybe an employee bio on the Regency website. But what popped up provided much more.

The first four hits for *Pauline Vick* were news articles from three years ago. The fifth was an article from a little over a year ago. The headlines told her everything she needed to know and she was almost afraid to click on the links. There might be answers there, but there was going to be a dark story as well.

"Jack, I got something," she said, still only looking at the headlines and links. "Something big, maybe."

"Yeah?"

"News articles from three years ago," she said. She finally opened the top result and read the article slowly, out loud, starting with the headline. "*Miracle Baby Delivered to 50 Year-Old Baltimore Woman.* For any woman, it becomes more and more difficult to conceive a child after the age of thirty-five," Rachel read. "After forty-five it is considered very difficult, and once you're north of fifty, it's practically unheard of. But that did not stop Pauline Vick, a local woman that currently works as a doctor at Regency Fertility Clinic. Pauline had been told since she and her late husband started trying to conceive in their early twenties that having a baby simply wasn't in the cards for them. 'I prayed and prayed about it,' Pauline said. But test after test kept telling me that it just wasn't going to happen. And then when my husband died five years ago, I nearly gave up. But I knew he'd want me to keep trying, so that's exactly what I did. I attempted in vitro, artificial insemination, the whole range of treatments. And then, last November, it happened. At the age of 49, I was pregnant!'"

Rachel scanned the rest of the article quickly. "You get the gist," she said.

"Sounds like an uplifting story," Jack said. "Why should that make me concerned."

"Because of another article from about a year and a half ago." She clicked on the article and this time, did not read it out loud. She scanned it and as she took the words in, she grew anxious and heartbroken at the same time.

"Read it for yourself," Rachel said, still processing it.

After a few moments, Jack set her phone down and said, "Jesus. The so-called miracle baby...died?"

"Three weeks shy of its first birthday," Rachel said. "Sudden infant death syndrome."

They said nothing for a moment, letting the heaviness of the news settle in. Rachel did her best to make absolutely sure this was something worth investigating She'd feel pretty fucking awful to bring such a painful point up to an innocent woman. But she could not see this as a coincidence. A woman that had been through that...who just happened to be a doctor at both clinics where it seemed women undergoing fertility treatments were being killed. It just couldn't be ignored.

"This is going to be rough," Jack said, getting up from the desk.

Rachel nodded her agreement, but she was already pulling up the number to Regency Fertility Clinic. The line was answered in her ear as they came to the doors of the station.

"Regency Fertility Clinic. How can I help you?"

Rachel said: "Yes, I'm looking for Doctor Pauline Vick."

"Dr. Vick?" the woman asked.

"Yes. Is that an issue?"

"Sort of. Dr. Pauline Vick hasn't worked here for about six weeks. She took a job with Baltimore Regional Hospital."

"Oh, I see. Do you happen to know if she's still running consults for Greenfield Women's Clinic?"

"Sorry, but no I don't."

Rachel ended the call and instantly pulled up the number for Baltimore Regional Hospital. As she put the call through, she looked to Jack and said, "Run a search for any criminal record. She's no longer with Regency and they couldn't tell me if she's stull doing consults." Just as Jack nodded, the line was answered, and Rachel did her best to be as polite and cheerful as possible. "Hello. This is Special Agent Rachel Gift. I'm currently in town on a case and I was hoping I could speak to a Dr. Pauline Vick. I understand that she's employed there currently."

"One moment," the receptionist said.

While on hold, Rachel looked over to Jack and saw that he was scrolling through the database for any information he could find on Pauline Vick. After several seconds, he shook his head and said: "Nothing here."

It took another minute or so for the receptionist to come back. When she did, she sounded very apologetic. "So sorry about the wait. She *is* on rotation today, but I'm told she's currently meeting with a patient. Can I take a message?"

Rachel considered it for a moment, but decided it would be best to take action rather than play phone tag. "That won't be necessary," she said. "But thank you."

CHAPTER TWENTY FOUR

When Rachel and Jack arrived at Baltimore Regional, Rachel could not help but feel that they were stuck in some sort of cyclone that kept them perpetually moving.

Rachel showed her badge as they approached. "I called about Dr. Vick about twenty minutes ago," she said. "It's very important that we speak to her as soon as possible."

"One moment," the receptionist said without any real spirit. She placed a call on her landline phone, waited, and then started speaking to someone on the other end, trying to locate Dr. Vick. When she was done, she looked back to Rachel and Jack with a rehearsed smile and said, "She's in one of the doctor's lounges right now, but she only has ten minutes before her next appointment."

"Any idea which lounge?" Jack asked.

"Dr. Vick is in prenatal, so it would most likely be the one all the way at the end of the third floor."

"Thanks so much," Rachel said, already moving away from the visitor's desk and toward the elevators.

As they were carried up to the third floor, Jack started thinking out loud—something he tended to do when they were actively on the hunt. "So Vick has access to both clinics and then conveniently gets a job somewhere new not too long before the murders start," he said. "It's not a smoking gun by any means, but it does seem a little suspicious, right?"

"A bit, yes." Rachel mulled it over, trying to look past the logic that told her a woman that was currently working in a prenatal program would probably be disgusted by the idea of someone killing women that were seeking out fertility treatments. Of course, Rachel had worked her fair share of cases where such reasoning had ended up serving as the killer's motive in the end. So she knew better than to rest her laurels on logic alone.

The elevator dinged and the doors slid open, revealing the third floor. As they walked down the hallway, it felt very much like the atmosphere of Regency clinic, only there were more men—husbands and boyfriends for the most part. Rachel saw several women sitting in a large waiting area in the center of the hallway, most of whom looked to be at least six or seven months pregnant.

"You know," Jack said, "as old-fashioned and caveman-like as it might sound, I don't know that men will ever feel comfortable in these places."

"Or any places that caters specifically to women," Rachel pointed out. "When I was pregnant with Paige, Peter *loathed* coming to my appointments. He did it because he was an awesome husband—came to every single appointment. But you could tell from the moment he stepped in the front door, he was very uncomfortable."

She tried to imagine Jack coming into a place like this, sitting in a room with a wife and many other uncomfortable women. But Jack had never married and really didn't even date all that much. She'd heard him mention a woman with any sort of real romantic interest one time and that had ended up coming to nothing.

"Something about this feels…right, I think," Jack said as the doctor's lounge drew closer. "You ever get that feeling that what you're about to step into might very well be what you're looking for?"

"On the job, yes," Rachel said. "In other aspects of life…rarely. And I'm getting something like that from Pauline Vick. But I think it might mostly be the awkwardness of the situation."

"I guess being the resident asshole comes with the job when you're an agent working on a case like this one, though," Jack said with a shrug.

When they were about twenty feet away from the lounge, a woman came walking out. She was dressed in a typical white doctor's vest and navy-blue pants. Rachel noted that the nametag on her chest read VICK. Pauline Vick was a short woman that looked quite athletic even under the long, white doctor's coat. Her black hair was pulled back in a tight ponytail and she looked as if someone had just called her every bad name they could think of.

"I assume you're the agents?" Pauline asked.

"Yes, ma'am, we are," Rachel said.

"I was paged and told I had two FBI agents here looking to speak with me," she said, confused. "Can I ask what this is in reference to?"

"We need some information from you regarding a case we're looking into," Rachel said. "Is there somewhere we can talk?"

"Well, I don't really have an office these days, so I think here in the hall will have to do. But as I'm sure the receptionist told you, I have an appointment with a patient in ten minutes so the hall might be for the best. Now…how can I help you?"

"Dr. Vick, have you heard about the three murders that have occurred in the city in the past few nights?" Rachel asked.

Slight confusion touched her features as she slowly said, "I'd heard that there were two women that had been killed. I was not aware there had been a third. One of the two was a woman I had consulted with just about two months ago."

"I assume that was before you got the job here at the hospital?" Rachel asked.

"Yes. I consulted with her at Greenfield. I take it you two are looking for the killer?"

"That's right. And so far, all we can gather is that somehow, the killer seems to know a list of women getting treatments, as well as when the treatments are scheduled and where they live."

Something like muted realization came over Dr. Vick's face. "Are you here to ask me about employees at the clinics? Do you really think someone that works at Regency or Greenfield would be a *killer?*"

The tone of Vick's voice changed drastically. She'd gone from meek and seemingly helpful to irate and angry in the space of about three seconds.

"Based on the facts as we know them," Jack said, "Yes, we have to assume that for right now. Currently, it's the only approach that seems fruitful."

"With all due respect, that's absurd. Please tell me you have not been harassing those poor doctors and nurses."

Rachel almost respected the way Pauline had communicated her grievance but there was an edge to it that honestly infuriated Rachel deep down. It wasn't necessarily a feeling of entitlement, but closer to a doctor *knowing* that these FBI agents were on *her* turf and finding a sense of skewed pride in that.

"No, we have not been *harassing* them," Rachel said. "But we have been questioning them to try to find some answers."

"So how do you think I can help you with your investigation?" Vick asked. "I can pretty much assure you that all of the women I have worked with at both of those clinics are one hundred percent absolutely *not* killers."

Rachel still tried to remind herself of the emotional trauma this woman had been through during her career—having to tell Lord only knew how many women that they would never be able to conceive a child; it certainly could not be an easy task. And then the poor woman's own horror story of having the so-called miracle baby after so much struggle and effort, only to lose it.

But she also had a case to close and she could not get past the suspicion that this doctor—who was visibly getting angrier and angrier—might very well be their killer.

"Well, let me repeat the facts as we know them," Rachel said. "Somehow, someone is not only targeting women because they are getting fertility treatments at these two clinics, but they also seem to know the dates the treatments are scheduled for. So, in addition to looking at patients that have familiarity with both clinics, we've also had to look at employees. And, as you might know, you're the only doctor in the past year or so that was floating back and forth between both clinics. You worked for Regency but also as something of a freelance consultant for Greenfield, right?"

"Yes, that's true. So if I can…"

"And then, just before the murders began, you picked up another job here."

Vick's brow furrowed and her jaw unhinged as she started to understand the purpose of their visit. She levelled her eyes at them in what was both pain and hatred. Rachel was able to keep her composure but had no clear idea of how to push forward. Thankfully, Jack stepped in. When he spoke, he sounded sincere and apologetic, but Rachel could tell that it was going to do no good.

"We know about your history," he said softly. "And while neither of us can imagine what it must have been like, we have to do our jobs. As FBI agents, we can't look past the coincidence of it all."

"Coincidence?" Pauline asked. It looked like she might scream or start weeping at any moment. "You mean my struggle to have a baby and then to lose it a year later? You think that makes me a killer?"

Her voice was getting louder and she took two steps closer toward them. One more step and she would literally be screaming right into Jack's face.

"Of course not," Jack said. He kept his own voice low and calm, trying his best to keep the situation from getting out of hand. "But it gives us more than enough reason to at least approach you to ask a series of questions. You can understand that, right?"

Pauline Vick's jaw was clenching and her eyes were starting to fill with tears. She did not blink as she stared them both down. She nodded slowly and with each nod of her head, Rachel saw more and more of the pain slipping away. All that was left was hatred. Rachel could almost feel it coming off of the woman in waves. She stood a little straighter in response, not sure what to expect.

113

"The personal hell I went through for more than fifteen years has nothing to do with your case or the workings of whatever madman you're after. The fact that you would even assume that I would have anything to do with it just because of personal pain is not only insulting, but so far beyond the realm of professionalism that it disgusts me."

"If you think we're enjoying this, you're sorely mistaken," Rachel said. "Based on countless case studies and research, people with severe trauma are far more likely to—"

It was then that Pauline Vick snapped. When it happened, it did so in a way that made Rachel think it had been a long time coming—that she and Jack just happened to be the one final push she'd needed. More than that, it made it just a bit easier to imagine this very same woman killing someone in a blind rage.

Pauline kicked at Jack and said: "Don't you *dare* talk to me about trauma!" Her foot glanced off of his shin and her volume got louder with each word. By the time she said *"trauma,"* she was screaming. "I've lived under this shadow for far too long and now to have it thrown in my face while I'm at work? *Are you fucking crazy?"*

Pauline swiped her hand out and forward in a fit of fury. She slapped at Jack's chest, though not in any real threatening way. Jack stepped back, raising his hands to show Pauline that he was not going to retaliate, that he meant her no harm.

"Dr. Vick, please—" was all Rachel was able to get out. When she realized that the next blow was going to be a side-swing fist directly to Jack's face, she moved instinctively. She was not able to block the blow completely, but she did catch Dr. Vick's right forearm as it struck Jack's chest.

Rachel applied just a bit of pressure and stepped forward She looked behind them and saw that at least five employees had stopped to see what was happening. Behind Vick, two people had come to peek their heads out of the doctor's lounge.

"Dr. Vick, you're attracting attention," Rachel hissed, still not letting go of her right arm. "You've struck an agent that did not physically provoke you, so you *will* be coming with us. It's up to you if we make it look really bad or as innocent as possible. This is *not* a threat, and I'll give you five seconds, right now, to decide."

She was clearly still furious but she nodded. "What about my appointments for the rest of the day?"

"You can use my phone to call and find someone to fill in," Rachel said. "But for now, you're coming with us."

Slowly, Rachel felt the fight go out of the woman's forearm. It felt like holding a stone that melted into jelly.

"You can't imagine…" Pauline said through clenched teeth and hitching breaths. "You can't do this…"

No refusing that she did it, Rachel thought. *No attempt to talk her way out of it. Maybe Jack was right…maybe this is the finish line.*

"Pauline Vick," Rachel said, "you are under arrest for suspicion of three murders."

She started to lead the woman right out of the office but figured she should save at least *some* dignity. "Jack, give me your jacket."

"What?"

"Jacket. Give it to me. Cuff her discreetly and hide it with your jacket."

He nodded and slipped out of his suit jacket. As he did, he also deftly took the cuffs from the little holstered section on the inside of the jacket. He cuffed her expertly and then draped the jacket over Pauline Vick's wrists. To anyone that was really paying close attention, it would still be pretty obvious what was happening—especially those that had all watched it go down right there in the third floor hallway. But so long as Pauline did not cause a scene out front, they should be okay.

Briefly, Rachel thought she felt the twinge of a headache, right behind her eyes. She waited a moment, terrified that she might be on the verge of another of her attacks. But the moment passed and she walked dutifully behind Pauline Vick as the three of them left the office and headed for the front doors.

CHAPTER TWENTY FIVE

Rachel was very glad this case wasn't going down in DC. If Director Anderson had been directly overseeing them, he would have raised all kinds of hell about them bringing in a woman that had lost a so-called miracle baby. He would have *understood* the reasoning behind it, but he would have still raised hell. For a man with such a temper at times, he tended to have a heart of gold.

But, of course, Director Anderson was not there. It was just her and Jack and they currently had a woman sitting at an interrogation room table—a woman that had lost a baby she had fought so hard to have. Not only that, but even after her horrors, a woman that continued to work with women with fertility issues on a daily basis.

Rachel knew she had a job to do but she also felt just a little bit like the scum of the earth as she and Jack walked into the interrogation room. Rachel took the single seat on their side of the table and gave Pauline a moment to compose herself. She'd been in the room for about seven minutes now and she did seem a bit more in control of herself than she had been in the car on the way to the precinct. She was still crying, but it was not the screaming of threats and the wailing about her past that she'd vented following her arrest.

Pauline started speaking, and Rachel would never have guessed what she said first.

"I'm sorry I kicked and punched you, Agent Rivers," Pauline said. "It was stupid, and I was barely even aware of what I was doing. As I'm sure you might understand, I get very defensive whenever someone asks me about what I've been through. But this...this was a whole new level..."

"No harm, no foul," Jack said. "I've had worse done to me. But what we need for you to tell us is *why* you acted the way you did."

"In that moment...in *every* moment when a reminder of what happened to me is somehow thrust into my face, my mind goes dark. Not *blank* but dark. There's this rage that comes over me and I'm usually able to contain it, thank God. And in the times I know I'm going to lose the fight against it, I can usually get out to my car and have a good cry, or I'm already at home and can break a few glasses in

116

the kitchen sink. But today I felt trapped, and I was already angry that I'd been paged twice to let me know you were there to see me."

"So it seems like the rage and darkness are temporarily at bay right now," Rachel said. "Is that right?"

"Yes."

"So now, with a mostly rational and clear mind, can you see why we would have to *at least* question you about these deaths based on the information we have on you?"

"It sucks, but yes. Yes, I understand. So go ahead and question me."

Rachel had seen people flip emotional switches like this before; the majority of the time, it was an act. She couldn't tell which was the case right now as Pauline Vick looked at them with tear-streaked cheeks and red, puffy eyes.

"It's actually pretty simple. The victims' names are—"

"Gloria Larsen, and Lucinda Masters," Pauline interrupted. "I know. Like I said, I'd heard about the first two. Who was the third?"

"Hannah Kettleman."

"You told us you'd consulted with one of them," Rachel asked. "Who was that?"

"I met with Gloria Larsen once, at Regency. It was more or less a consult when her original doctor was away at the hospital for an emergency."

"And how well do you remember her?" Jack asked.

"Not well, honestly. It was one of those long days where everyone you see sort of blends together. I just remember that she was going through some simple tests to make sure she was viable for one of the treatment options."

"What about Lucinda Masters and Hannah Kettleman?" Rachel asked "Had you at least *heard* of them before their murders?"

"Not that I can recall."

Rachel leaned forward, kicking in one of the little subtle indicators she had Jack had come up with. Whenever she leaned forward intentionally, Jack knew to study the suspect's eyes. It meant Rachel was about to ask a leading or blunt question. And Jack, always good at reading expressions, was to watch the suspect's face carefully.

"Where were you on the last several nights?" she asked. "Give us ten days. Can you tell us where you were when the murder occurred?"

"I don't know," she said, clearly starting to get defensive now. "I'm not exactly sure *when* they occurred."

Jack flipped through the folder on the table and pulled out one of the sheets. "Gloria Larsen, five days ago, estimated time of death around six in the afternoon. Lucinda Masters, three days ago, likely around two in the morning. Hannah Kettleman, yesterday, time of death undetermined but likely somewhere between eleven at night and two in the morning."

Something flickered in Pauline's eyes—a bit of uneasiness that Rachel caught. It was almost like the look of someone considering a bluff in a suddenly serious game of poker.

"For Gloria Larsen, I would have either been on my way home from the hospital or still there, wrapping paperwork from my last appointment. I don't know for sure. For the other two, I was at home asleep."

"Do you have any proof?" Jack asked.

"Proof that I was at home, asleep?"

"Yes. Security cameras, maybe? Anything like that?"

Rachel applauded him for not mentioning a spouse, as the articles they'd read specifically mentioned how her husband had died five years ago. No need in giving her another emotional slap in the face while accusing her of murder.

"No. As for the first murder, I can have my computer checked to see when I logged out that day."

"Would you allow us to look at your phone, or are you going to make us get a warrant?" Jack asked.

"You could," Pauline said. "But it's in my purse, back at Greenfield. You sort of escorted me out before I had a chance to mention it."

Rachel thought for a good twenty seconds, sure that Jack might interject at some point. When he didn't, Rachel asked a question that she figured might very well piss Pauline off, but she had to take the chance. It would not only do a great deal in showing Pauline's level of honesty, but could also serve as a trap of sorts. If she *was* the killer, it was the type of question that presented a minefield of danger for her.

"Dr. Vick, how is it that you're still able to work with pregnant women after al you've been through? Doesn't it affect you mentally?"

Pauline gave her a vicious look which she managed to temper just before she opened her mouth in response. "There are days when it is very hard," she said, speaking slowly and barely opening her mouth. "There are days when I want to quit. But I remember that feeling of absolute bliss and triumph when I was finally able to conceive, and it pushes me through. I took the job at the hospital because I'm now working with women that are already pregnant. It's a massive difference and helped me get away from the darker, depressing things."

"Back at Regency and Greenfield, did you ever resent the women that had successful treatments?" Jack asked.

"Of course I did," Pauline said. "No point in lying about that. But I stored it up. I stored it up and swallowed it down."

"And it comes out in anger," Rachel said.

"Yes. And until today, I've managed to keep it hidden and under control."

Or have you? Rachel wondered. *Maybe it's also been coming out in the brutal murders of these three women.*

"We need to hold you for a bit," Rachel said. "We'll send an officer back over to the hospital to retrieve your purse and phone. Plus, there's also the matter of you assaulting a federal agent."

Pauline sighed deeply and rolled her eyes in what almost came off as the expression of an annoyed teenager. Rachel supposed it was worlds better than chucking a laptop at an FBI agent, though.

Rachel stood up from her chair and stepped outside. Jack followed her out into the hallway and they walked slowly back toward their little work station.

"Thoughts?" Jack asked.

"I think if her phone and her work computer can't provide an alibi, she's a very strong suspect. The motive is there, and based on the last hour or so, I'd say she'd be considered somewhat emotionally sporadic at best."

"Agreed," Jack said. "Seems like this might be the killer, though, right?"

"Maybe so," Rachel said. "For now, let's get someone to get her phone and work computer so we can find out."

CHAPTER TWENTY SIX

A very excited-looking policeman rushed to the desk Rachel and Jack had been calling home. He was carrying Pauline Vick's purse under one arm, carrying it pretty much the same way Rachel had always seen men carrying a purse. She'd always teased Peter about the way he held hers whenever she had to hand it over to him for some reason or another. He'd always hold it out in front of him, as if his arm might catch on fire if it even accidentally brushed his shoulder.

"Thanks, officer," Jack said as he took the purse.

They both looked inside and found her phone. There was little else there to support the theory that she might be the killer, though. The cop that dropped it off watched on, as if he, too, wanted to share in whatever discovery they made. Pity for him, there was nothing.

"There was no actual work laptop to take," the officer explained. "Because Dr. Vick is rather new to the hospital and shares her station, she also shares a laptop with three other doctors. She does have her own smart tablet, though. It was through that where I was able to find out that the hospital can confirm that she logged out from work at 5:37 on the day Gloria Larsen was killed."

This did provide Rachel and Jack with at least one new tidbit of news. Based on the distance between Regency and the Larsen's residence, it would have been very possible for Pauline to travel from work, directly to their residence to kill Gloria. As a matter of fact, based on the estimated time of death, there would have been more than enough time, so long as Pauline worked quickly.

It was a small crumb, but it felt significant. Yet, even as the local PD's techs unlocked Pauline's phone and started to study the GPS movements of the past few weeks, Rachel started to feel something nagging at the back of her mind—not anything Pauline Vick had said, but something Alex Lynch had told her.

I would assume, then, that the killer has nothing personal against the women...

If that was true, then Pauline Vick may not be their killer after all. She'd even come out and admitted that she sometimes resented the women that she saw. That, plus helping them along with their treatments gave them a pretty close and personal connection.

So, then what's missing? Rachel wondered. *Or was Alex Lynch wrong? Was he feeding me a line of bullshit just to mess with me?*

She didn't think this was the case, though. In fact, the more she thought about that one comment, the more sense it made. Based on a few cases from her past, she knew that the majority of the time a murder case where the victim and murderer knew one another, there was usually some sort of significance or personal touch to it. And that was missing here.

Still waiting on the results from Pauline's phone, Rachel thought of any other connections the victims might have. If they'd all seen Pauline Vick at some point, that might actually make for a pretty secure case. But Pauline had only seen Hannah...a fact that they could verify through the lists they'd gotten from the clinics.

Yet, as she looked at the records, there was one more similarity that stood out. It may not mean anything, but she wasn't sure, as she wasn't very well-versed on fertility treatments. The records showed that all three women had been scheduled for IVF treatments. Rachel did know enough to realize that meant donor eggs would be fertilized in a laboratory and then implanted into the patient's uterus.

In other words, all three women would have required donor eggs.

Rachel's mind started to spin. It was one of those links that seemed like a stretch at first but the more she sat on it, the more relevant it seemed.

"Hey, Jack, how much do you know about IVF treatments?"

Jack looked up from the laptop and frowned at her. "Sadly, I don't know if this is some sort of trick question."

"It's not. But I'm wondering...each woman would have needed donor eggs for their treatments."

"All three of them were undergoing the same sort of treatment?"

"Yeah, it seems that way," Rachel said, tapping the sheets of paper that confirmed this. "And from what I understand, it's a rather popular treatment but...still. It seems sort of odd, right?"

"I don't know. Sorry...I'm going to be the idiot male here. What's an IVF treatment?"

"In vitro fertilization. Taking an egg into a laboratory and trying to fertilize it with donated sperm."

Jack wrinkled his nosy playfully and shook his head. "So now I know. Anyway...you think that might be important?"

"I don't know. But what I do know is that I want a backup plan already in place if the techs come up with nothing from her phone."

Rachel had already picked up the phone and was pulling up the number for Regency. She was sure she'd spoken to the woman that had answered before at some point but wasn't positive. She felt like she'd called and visited about a trillion times so far.

"This is Agent Gift," Rachel said. "I need to get some information about donor eggs for the case I'm currently working on."

"What sort of information?" the receptionist asked.

"If possible, I need to know the names of the women that donated eggs that could have ended up going to the victims."

The receptionist waited a moment and when she finally answered, it was a tone that indicated she was getting pretty tired of visits and calls from the FBI. "Well, I certainly can't give you that information and I can tell you with pretty strong confidence that even if a doctor here *would* provide that information, they'd tell you to come visit. It's not the sort of thing anyone is going to give out over the phone."

"Fine. Would it be Mrs. Carpenter again?"

"Yes."

"Could you please let her know I'm on my way over then? Again."

"Yes, I can tell her but I don't know what the rest of her schedule looks like for the day."

"I'll take the chance," Rachel asserted as she got to her feet and ended the call.

"Need me to come along?" Jack asked.

"No, it's okay. One of us should be here when the techs have results on Pauline Vick's phone. This shouldn't take long."

"Happy hunting," Jack said, looking back to the laptop.

Rachel wished it were just her imagination but as she left, she was pretty sure Jack was glancing at her over the laptop—no doubt still trying to figure out what was going on with her.

Or maybe you're just imagining it, she told herself. She did not realize it until that very moment, but she was starting to think of this voice as the Tumor. *Maybe you feel like he's watching you because you're lying to him just like you're lying to your family. Guilt is a bitch, isn't it?*

Yes, apparently it was. And though she was going back to the clinic by herself, she almost felt like the pressing presence of guilt and fear was now going to be a constant passenger.

***

Rachel did her best to hide her irritation as she walked quickly to the entrance doors of Regency Fertility Clinic. She noticed there were no protestors today, wondering if word had gotten around about the arrest of one of their ilk. As she pushed through the doors and walked inside, she also tried reminding herself that the women here at Regency had very stressful jobs to do and what may seem like a lack of cooperation likely just came down to making sure the private information of their patients and donors were kept confidential.

She knew all of this, of course, but it was hard to keep it in focus with three dead bodies and her own medical situation to contend with.

To her surprise, Mrs. Carpenter was already waiting for her. She was standing behind one of the reception cubicles. When she saw Rachel heading her way, Carpenter headed around to little desk to meet her.

"This way, please," Carpenter said, not bothering with hellos.

She led Rachel down the central hallway and came to a small office just short of the waiting room. She closed the door softly behind them and took a seat behind the single desk in the room. There were no additional chairs for Rachel to sit in.

"I want to start," Carpenter said, "by letting you know that I've heard about what happened with Pauline Vick. I find it outrageous and borderline ridiculous. That woman has been through hell and I can't imagine what she's going through right now."

"It's not a decision we made lightly," Rachel said, not liking that she felt as if she had to defend herself.

"I can tell you with no hesitancy at all that Pauline Vick is not a killer. I've known her for the better part of ten years and watched her go through each and every painful step of being unable to conceive, losing her husband, and then finally getting pregnant and losing that child."

"I would love nothing more than for you to be right," Rachel said. "And that's why we're here. I'm tracking one final thing, one lead that may help to—"

"I was told you want a list of egg donor names."

"That's right."

"Well, there are a lot of donors. We have more than sixty. And there is no selective process to figure out which recipient gets which egg. So, I can't weed out the list like that."

Rachel nodded, once again trying to slip herself into a killer's mindset. She thought of Alex Lynch sitting across from her in the visitation room, those manic eyes drilling holes into her. She thought of the hatred it must take to do what he did, the absolute lack of empathy. It brought up another question, one she was still considering when she asked it.

"I'm curious," Rachel said. "Are there women that ever regret the decision to donate eggs? Have you ever had a woman come back and ask to have the eggs destroyed?"

Even before the question was out, Rachel knew that she'd potentially stumbled upon something. She could see it in Mrs. Carpenter's face.

"It's very rare," Carpenter said, "but as it just so happens, there was a woman that made this request a few weeks ago. Three weeks, to be exact."

Bingo, Rachel thought. She stepped toward the desk, her eyes locked on Carpenter. "And how did that go?"

"Not well," Carpenter said. Her tone indicated that she realized that she may have just opened up something of a Pandora's Box. Without asking to explain, she did so willingly. "A woman approached the front desk and didn't even ask for a specific doctor. From what I'm told, she was very polite when she asked the receptionist how she could go about getting her eggs back or having them destroyed. When the receptionist told her that's not exactly how it worked, the polite mask went away quickly. Of course, the receptionist should have never commented on it and had the woman speak with a doctor, but that is neither here nor there. The woman sort of snapped. I only caught the end of it, but you can see it on one of our security feeds. I would not be exaggerating to say that this woman threw a tantrum. She was banging on the protective glass between the desk and the receptionist. One of our ladies up front had picked up the phone to call the police but by then, the woman seemed to come to her senses."

Rachel wondered if the woman had displayed the same sort of anger that would drive someone to repeatedly stab three women in the stomach.

"What's the woman's name?" Rachel asked.

"Claire Allen. And I think I should probably add that one of the many things she yelled while she was here was that we were just as clueless and as mean as the other clinic."

"The *other* clinic? You mean Greenfield?"

"Yes. I had someone here call to warn them about her but they said she'd already been there. She wasn't quite as confrontational to them, but yes…she had also visited Greenfield to have them destroy her donated eggs as well."

Rachel could feel the case sliding together in her head, all the puzzle pieced interlocking. This was not a traumatized doctor being questioned in a hospital hallway, snapping after years of pain. This was something different. There was a slight edge of madness to this, a woman raising hell because a clinic would not "give her back" her eggs.

"I need her phone number and address," Rachel said.

It was clear that Carpenter was uneasy with it, but she typed something into her laptop without much hesitation. After a few clicks and a couple taps of her keyboard, she grabbed a Post It and a pen from beside the laptop.

"Here you go," she said, tearing the information off of the stack and handing it to Rachel. "I do hope you can wrap this…not just to catch the killer, but to finally stop going after women like Pauline Vick."

Rachel saw it as an unnecessary jab, but said nothing. She gave a little nod of appreciation and made her exit. The tiny piece of paper she held in her hand started to feel as heavy as a brick and by the time she was at the exit doors, she was almost running to her car.

CHAPTER TWENTY SEVEN

It was 4:40 when Rachel pulled out of the Regency parking lot and placed a call to Jack. It rang three times before he answered, making her think that he and the techs might have found something in regards to the GPS locations on Pauline's phone.

"Find anything?" Jack asked.

"Oh, I think I did. I think I might have found our killer."

"Are you serious?" he said. "Just like that?"

"Just like that."

He laughed and when he did, Rachel could imagine him giving one of his comical little fist pumps—not just for the good news but because it would not be the first time during their partnership that Rachel and come across a potentially case-ending lead without his help.

"That's great," he said, "but it makes us look like fools for the poor lady we currently have waiting in an interrogation room. I'll say, though...I hope you do have a promising lead. There's nothing on Pauline's phone to indicate that she knew the victims or that she'd been anywhere near their homes."

"That doesn't rule her out completely, Jack. She could have been very careful, you know."

"But I thought you said you had maybe found our killer...as in it's not Vick."

"I feel like you're intentionally being irritating."

"Maybe."

"Look, I'll be at the station in about fifteen minutes. While I'm on my way, I need you to run a search on a woman named Claire Allen. Criminal record, job history, everything you can get."

"Jesus...what happened?"

Rachel was driving fast, careening around cars on the four-lane and blasting through yellow-and-soon-to-be-red lights. She set her phone to speaker mode, set it in the center console, and told him everything Mrs. Carpenter had just told her about Claire Allen. It didn't take long but somehow, she had already closed in on the last mile or so before she'd reach the station.

"Okay, yeah, that sounds promising," Jack said. "I've got a few things pulled up right now. Want me to read it all to you?"

"No. Print as much as you can out and meet me in front of the station in about five minutes."

Rachel ended the call and her mind instantly went back to Alex Lynch. She knew it was foolish and perhaps even a bit naïve to think that all killers thought the same, operated the same, and had the same lack of a moral code. But those hardened eyes still seemed to peer at her from across that interrogation room. They read her and, in turn, told her that there were secrets behind those eyes—a secret understanding of people that thought the same way he did.

She wondered if they would be so close to the end of this case if she had not thought to go to him. It had seemed like such an extreme measure at the time but now she doubted she would have made some of the connections she'd made without the visit. It almost made her feel like she was indebted to him now and that made it so much worse.

She arrived at the station just a few moments later, and Jack was waiting for her with a folder in his hand. Rachel barely brought the car to a stop at all as she pulled up in front of the building and Jack got in.

"Put this address into your GPS, would you?" Rachel asked, handing him the Post It Mrs. Carpenter had given her.

Jack took the paper and typed the address in right away. While the directions loaded, he flipped the folder open. Rachel saw that there were only three pages and the first one did not contain much information at all.

"Claire Allen, age thirty-nine, and a Baltimore resident. Previously employed at a variety of different department stores but most recently employed at J. Jenkins School for the Gifted. No real criminal record to speak of, just a drug bust for pot when she was twenty and three speeding tickets over the last ten years."

"Married?" Rachel asked.

"No. Not from what I can see here."

The robotic female voice from Jack's phone told Rachel to take the next right and then to get off on the connector highway that would lead to the interstate. "How much longer before we get there?" Rachel asked.

"Twenty-two minutes."

They both sat in the excitement of the moment, though Rachel spent most of that time wondering if this was a connection they should have made on their own. As much as she would like to take the credit, she'd always know that it had been her conversation with Alex that had brought them here. And she was going to have to live with that—no matter how the case turned out.

Rachel also wondered why the eventual climax of this case seemed to sit heavier on her chest than most others she'd closed. She was excited to get there, to confront the killer and get the hell back home. But why?

You know why, she told herself. Or rather, maybe it was the Tumor speaking up again. *Because this secret tumor of yours is eating you alive in more ways than one. Whether or not you want to admit it, you know you need to tell Peter. You have to tell Peter, Paige, Jack, Director Anderson...everyone. And you can't very well do that while you're in Baltimore, hunting a killer, now can you?*

"Rachel?"

Jack's voice brought her out of her thoughts. She snapped to attention and said, "Yeah?"

"The robot lady said turn up here! Didn't you hear?"

"Shit. Sorry."

She had *not* heard, as she'd been too lost in her own thoughts. She sped up a bit to cut off the car beside her and slid into the exit lane. She was aware of Jack giving her a concerned look, but she didn't acknowledge it. She waited for one of his *"get your shit together"* comments but, for the second time she'd been expecting it, he remained quiet. And when the GPS voice told her to take a left at the fork as she came to the end of the ramp, she did so without missing a beat.

"Rachel?" Jack said, his voice low and rather sudden.

"What?"

"Don't bullshit me. What's wrong with you? What's going on?"

"Are you really going to pull this with me again? Right now?"

"Yeah. You're zoning out...you're not *really* here most of the time. And where the hell did you take off to for a few hours yesterday?"

She was surprised how easily she came out with the truth. Even as she said it, she realized she was telling *this* truth to make up for the much larger truth she was keeping from him.

"I went to see Alex Lynch."

He stared at her blankly for a moment, perhaps waiting for her to say, *"just kidding."* When it was clear she wasn't about to say any such thing, he said: "You did *what?*"

She shrugged as if it were no big deal, keeping her eyes on the road. "There were things about this case that reminded me of him and I couldn't get away from it. He kept popping up in my mind and...I don't know. I figured it might help me personally *and* with this case."

"Rachel, that's...that's nuts. I mean, what the hell were you thinking?"

"I just explained what I was thinking."

"Please tell me you did not reveal details of a case to a serial killer."

"Nothing major, no."

He went quiet again and though she was not looking at him, she could sense his disapproval. "My God, Rachel. How could you...I mean, you know that anything he might have told you was likely bullshit, right?"

"Right. But it...it sort of cleared a few things up." This hurt to admit, and she wanted nothing more than for Jack to drop it. He didn't, though.

"It just makes no sense, Rachel. I know you went to see him those few times not long after he was sentenced, but...have there been any other times?"

"No. Just yesterday."

"And...well, are you okay?"

She couldn't bring herself to say anything. Saying *yes* would be a lie. So she settled for a nod and that seemed to be enough for him. He said nothing else, and Rachel focused every bit of her attention on the road ahead so she would not have to look at him. In doing so, Rachel realized they had just barely missed the gridlock of evening traffic. That, she supposed, was something to be thankful for. It was 5:21, so perhaps they had just barely squeaked out ahead of it. A few minutes later, when the GPS voice told her to take a right and that her destination would be on the left just half a mile ahead, that stirring of excitement in her guts intensified. She legitimately could not remember the last time she'd been so hyped up to confront the person at the end of such a promising lead.

She took the turn when it came and as they neared Claire Allen's address, she noticed Jack sitting rigidly in his seat. He was clenching and unclenching his fists and bobbing his head like he was listening to music that only he could hear. She wondered if her excitement was rubbing off on him.

It turned out that Claire Allen lived in a small cluster of townhouses. There were more townhomes being built to the right of the property, and a scant grove of trees blocking the property from the incredibly busy road to the left. The address gave her townhouse number as 108, and the agents approached it with restrained promise.

When Rachel knocked on the door, her heart seemed to hammer right along with it. There was no answer, so after ten seconds, she knocked again. She knocked significantly harder this time and even added in quite loud, "Ms. Allen? Hello?"

After another handful of seconds of silence, it was clear that she either wasn't home or simply not answering the door.

"It *is* creeping up on five thirty," Jack said. "She could be on her way home from work, stuck in afternoon traffic."

"Could be," Rachel said. "But this killer is working fast. And based on the timeline we have so far, unless she's decided to stop out of nowhere, she's due to strike either tonight or tomorrow night."

"But we don't have any idea who the next victim might be."

"We *might* be able to figure it out. How many more women on that Facebook group were local to the Baltimore area?"

Jack grinned at her, pointing to her in the way an excited coach might point to a player that had just made a great play. "Two more."

"Well, if the group is now closed and the killer maybe kept a list, they'd still have the names. I think it's a safe bet one of those two women is next. And being that Claire Allen isn't home…"

"We need to hurry," Jack finished for her, already reaching for his phone as he and Rachel ran back to the car.

***

She'd almost screwed up.

She got to the house a little early. She'd thought the husband would be gone by the time she parked across the street, but he was still there. She had been fairly certain the husband left for his night shift at six in the afternoon…but it was apparently six-thirty. She was usually very good with details like that. She figured it was the presence of the police that was affecting her—not only her ability to retain facts she had drilled into her head about her victims, but also her nerves. This made no real sense, though; ever since she'd heard the news that some poor doctor had been arrested in regards to the murders, she'd felt more relaxed and at ease. They had someone else in custody, so she was in the clear. Apparently, they'd never even been close to finding her.

That meant there was no rush. She could wait. She had to get this one exactly right because it looked like this would be the last victim. Until she figured out where to easily find more victims, this woman would be the last. She looked out to the house—to the McNeil residence. It was a lovely two-story home, right in the middle of a well-to-do (though not wealthy) suburb. The grass had been mowed recently, probably the first time of the season, as summer had not truly settled in just yet. An attached garage sat on the left, with a rectangular slab of concrete leading out onto the street.

She sat patiently in her car, slightly slouched but not enough to look suspicious. Hell, it was getting dark out now, so maybe it would work in her favor that she'd gotten the time wrong. She could wait...though her nerves made her wonder if this was really the case.

She eased up a bit at 6:23, when the garage door opened up. She could just barely hear it through her window, a slight mechanical whir as the door was rolled up. She watched as the husband's Ford F150 rolled back out onto the street. She knew it would turn right and head out to the exit of the little subdivision. From there, it would take the seventeen-mile drive to Wagner Textiles, where the husband worked as a floor manager. She knew this because, like all of the other victims, she had done her research.

She waited exactly five minutes, making sure the husband did not turn around because he'd forgotten something. Night had almost totally fallen over the city now, but not quite. When she walked across the street, her shadow was stretched and fuzzy against the street lights. Insects flickered and dived around it, but she barely noticed. She was heading to the side of the house, where the small picket-fence style gate separated the back yard from the side yard. A tall line of shrubs also separated the McNeil house from the neighbors' yard.

She knew the gate was busted, though. There was a lock, but it was mostly for decoration. She reached over the short gate, having to stand on the tips of her toes, and unlatched the lock. It swung open and granted her access to the back yard. Here, she pressed herself to the side of the house and inched to the porch. She took the steps slowly, knowing that the third one from the bottom creaked. Finally on the porch, she walked to very edge of the window that looked into the kitchen. She closed her eyes and listened and yes, sure enough, there it was. Cassie McNeil was a creature of habit, that was for sure. She'd cut on some '90s rock and had already brought the canvas and the paints out to the kitchen table. She'd been working on a seascape for the past few nights, the canvas held by a cheap, small easel that she placed on the kitchen table. Truth be told, it wasn't all that bad.

The current song playing was "No Rain" by Blind Melon. She watched Cassie McNeil paint for a moment. She was putting a bit of detail onto a gray cloud. Apparently, there was a storm out at sea.

As the song hit the second chorus, she looked away from the painting and started slowly inching herself towards the door.

She slowly took the knife out of the waist of her pants with her left hand as her right reached for the doorknob.

Yes, there was a storm coming for sure. Just not the sort Cassie McNeil was dreaming up less than fifteen feet away.

CHAPTER TWENTY EIGHT

"I forgot that the fucking group was set to Private," Jack said. "I can't get to the names anymore. I just messaged the admin, but their little status dot is telling me they aren't online."

"Didn't you have a hand-written list back at the station?"

"Yeah, I do," he said, pulling up the number to the station and placing the call. He set the phone on the console and set it to speaker mode. "I just hope I didn't miss anything…"

When the woman at the dispatch desk answered, Jack cut her off in the middle of her introduction.

"This is Agent Rivers. I need someone to rush back to the desk my partner and I have been using and find a name for me."

"Of course," the woman said. "I can do that for you right now. What do you need?"

"There's a list of names scribbled down, labelled *Family Focus Fertility, Baltimore*. There should only be a few names on it that are not crossed out. I need those names."

"Sure, sure," the woman said. The rustling of the phone and the woman's labored breathing made it clear that she was on the move.

Rachel had brought the car to the end of the townhouse parking lot, not sure which direction to go. The feeling of anxiousness roared up inside of her again. She did not believe in things like signs or intuitive feelings but she could not deny that she suddenly felt like she and Jack were currently racing the clock—that a woman's life very well could be hanging in the balance.

"Okay, Agent Rivers?" the woman on the other end said. "I see it right here. And there are only two names that had not been crossed through. One is Jessie Dugger. The other is Cassie McNeil."

"Okay, I need another favor," Jack said. "Use the laptop right there at the desk and get on the network. I need addresses for both of those women as soon as you can get them."

"Okay…"

The woman was clearly rattled, apparently feeling the tension in Jack's voice as it tore through the phone lines. In the silence of the car, they could hear the muted clicking from the other line. Rachel had her phone ready, prepared to plug the addresses into her GPS.

"Okay, I've got an address for Jessie Dugger as 609 Montgomery Street. Now for Cassie McNeil…"

Rachel plugged the Montgomery Street address in and found that it was twenty-one miles away. She waited for the next one, thumbs poised and ready.

"…1612 Lavender Avenue."

Rachel typed the address in and found that this one was significantly closer—just thirteen miles away. "Ma'am, this is Agent Rachel Gift," she said. "Agent Rivers and I are going to take the Lavender Avenue address. To save some time, I need you to send a car out to the Dugger residence as well. We have reason to believe a woman's life is in danger."

"Oh…okay…I…"

"If there are any issues, just have them call this number," Jack said. He then recited his phone number slowly as Rachel turned out onto the road, heading back out toward the interstate and in the direction of the McNeil residence.

***

Cassie had never painted anything other than flat colors on bedroom walls until about three years ago. Her doctor had suggested it as a means to get over her anxiety. He'd advised that she start with paint-by-numbers sets at first, but that got boring very quickly. Then, one Saturday morning—having just received another batch of bad news concerning fertility treatments the day before—Cassie had gone to Hobby Lobby and purchased about one hundred dollars' worth of paint and supplies. She'd then found a few basic tutorials on YouTube and by that night, she was hooked.

She'd worked on honing her craft and now the tutorials she watched were much more advanced. She was even paying a subscription fee to one artist's channel and she knew she had gotten much better. She was still just as anxious these days now that she was being told there was a very good chance she'd be able to conceive via IVF treatments.

Because good news often made her stress even worse (thinking of all the ways it could go wrong) she'd been painting a lot over the past two weeks. Four ocean scenes, a generic still-life of the birdhouse in the backyard, and now tonight's project—finishing a seascape. There was no land, just the crashing of waves during the beginning of a storm at sea.

It only took a few brush strokes to get her there—into a nearly hypnotic state where her stress and anxiety became little more than a blur on the canvas in front of her. She had Spotify open on her phone, listening to a playlist of her favorite '90s alternative tracks. She blended navy-blue and white, adding in a bit of green and just a dab of white, trying to get the right color for the caps of the smaller waves. Applying it to the canvas, it came out too dark, so she wetted her brush, got a little bit more white, and started fixing it up.

She wasn't sure how long she'd bene painting when she heard the noise at the back door. It was far too easy for Cassie to lose herself in her painting. There had been nights when her husband was at work when she'd start painting around seven and somehow it would be midnight before she even bothered to look at the digital clock on the microwave.

She placed her brush down on the table and turned to the door. It was opening, which caused her heart to slam in her chest, and then someone entered her house.

"Who are—"

Those were the only words that came out of her mouth before the crazed-looking woman came rushing across the kitchen. Cassie didn't see the knife in the woman's hand until the very last second and even then, as she backed against the kitchen table and heard her brushed clinking in the water jar, she was pretty sure it was too late.

CHAPTER TWENTY NINE

Rachel did eighty-five the whole way there, cutting off several people and receiving a chorus of blaring horns as she merged off of the interstate. When she came to the small subdivision, she nearly slammed into the side of a parked car on the curb. She saw Jack cringing from his place in the passenger seat and understood that he wasn't simply being dramatic; she wasn't sure she'd ever driven so recklessly before.

It was 6:41 when she pulled the car up in front of the McNeil house. The street lights illuminated the mostly darkened streets. As they got out of the car, the neighborhood was quiet with the exception of a dog barking somewhere nearby. Even further away, almost like a ghost, Rachel could hear two kids laughing about something.

They hurried to the front porch, Jack taking the lead. They quietly made their way up the stairs and Jack wasted no time knocking on the door. Almost right away, there was a commotion from inside. It was hard to tell through the closed door, but to Rachel there was a noise that sounded almost like a windchime, and then the sound of glass breaking.

Just as Rachel and Jack shared a concerned look, there was another noise: a woman's muffled cry of pain and surprise.

Rachel tried the door but found it locked. Jack ushered her to the side, took two large strides backwards, and then delivered a vicious kick to the door. It gave, but not quite enough. But on Jack's second attack, it went flying inward, sending small chunks of the doorframe with it.

It was one of those moments where neither of them yelled out to announce their presence. The commotion they'd heard through the door had been more than enough. As they'd done in the past in such a situation, they split up to cover more ground in the event the suspect made a run for it. Rachel headed straight into the house while Jack ran off of the porch and made his way around the house to find the back door.

Rachel strode inside and found herself stepping straight into a large living room. It was mostly tidy, but with signs of recent use: a pair of discarded shoes, an empty glass on the coffee table. She heard more noises from the back of the house. It was that same windchime-like sound and what was obviously the sound of a skirmish of some kind.

She ran through the hallway and came to a neat, modest kitchen. Or so it seemed. There was a strange gray sort of water on the floor, and shattered glass. Rachel's eyes saw all of this first, but then saw the two women pressed against the far wall. The woman that was losing the battle was pressed against the wall, her bare feet kicking along the floor for traction, kicking up the gray water. The woman was bleeding from a wound along her side. And even as Rachel watched, she saw the attacker draw a knife backward, intending to drive it forward. But in the midst of the attacker's frenzy, she saw Rachel enter the room. Rachel had her Glock out and raised it. The killer stopped, smiled, and then held the knife to the woman's throat.

"Drop the knife, Mrs. Allen."

"No. I planned so hard for this. This is…this is the only way I can…"

"It's too late, Mrs. Allen. I spoke with the people at Regency. It has nothing to do with you or your situation. And neither does this woman."

Claire looked genuinely confused for a moment, shaking her head. "But I have to have my chance back. It's not fair…"

"You donated the eggs, right?" Rachel asked.

For a moment, Rachel thought the confusion and distraction was going to allow Cassie McNeil to slip free from Claire's clutches. But the woman's grip was apparently quite strong.

"I did. I wanted the money and I thought I may as well see if someone else could be fortunate and have a child. But I…I couldn't stand the thought of it."

"You visited other women, too, right? Three others?"

Claire nodded matter-of-factly, as if she honestly didn't see what the big deal was. But Rachel saw the strength in her wrist as she held the knife to Cassie McNeil's throat. One quick motion was all it would take.

"Mrs. Allen, you've been through a lot, haven't you?" Rachel asked.

She nodded and her face started to grow red as tears slipped from the corners of her eyes. As Claire struggled with this, Rachel could see the murky shape of Jack out on the back porch. He was peering in through the window, and she gave him a quick shake of the head. *Not yet,* that shake of the head said. For now, she felt she had things at least somewhat under control. The sudden appearance of another armed agent might drive Claire Allen to slide that knife right into Cassie McNeil's neck.

"Just put the knife away," Rachel said. "Whatever your pain is, it did not come from this woman. She doesn't even know you. And the same was true of the other women. You understand that, right?"

For a brief moment, Rachel thought that had done it; she thought she saw the knife coming away and a sort of relaxed posture come over Claire. But as soon as it appeared, it was gone. She pressed even harder against Cassie and screamed: "But my eggs...*my eggs* that I had donated...why should some other woman be able to use what was *rightfully mine?*"

Rachel eyed Jack through the window, hoping he hadn't taken Claire's screaming as a cue to come in. He still stood there, looking as if he were spring loaded and ready to jump.

"Mrs. Allen, drop the knife. If you have any hope for a way out of this, you need to drop the...the knife..."

Without any warming at all, Rachel felt herself growing light-headed. A thin streak of white darted across her vision, followed by a larger one.

No...no...not now...

She did her best to keep her feet but swayed forward a bit. She felt herself falling forward, her mind going faint and hazy. And apparently Claire Allen saw this as an aggressive move.

The good news was that she removed the knife from Cassie's throat as she redirected her attention at Rachel. Claire lunged hard to the right and slashed out quickly. She missed Rachel by about a foot, but kept coming even in her failed attack. As Rachel stumbled forward, still reeling and not quite there, Claire slammed into her.

Rachel was thrown back into one of the chairs around the kitchen table. As her legs tangled with it, she caught a glimpse of where the gray water was coming from. There was a painting-in-progress on the table, knocked loose from its canvas. Somewhere during the killer's attack the water used to clean the brushes had been knocked over and rolled to the floor where it shattered. Another glass jar with brushes had rolled over on the table, making the windchime sound Rachel had heard. It all looked vague and abstract as her vision blurred.

This quick summary of the scene was caught in a split second as she fell to the floor. And when she hit the floor, she realized it might have been the best thing that could have happened. The impact knocked some of the wind out of her and seemed to bring her mind back around to the pressure of the moment. There was one final hazy streak of white and then her vision started to clear up. The veil of blackness was slowly pushed away.

The first thing her now-clear vision saw was Claire Allen swiping the knife down towards her. Rachel brought her forearm up in a desperate defensive move and slammed it into Claire's chin. Claire was rocked and as she tottered backwards, Rachel caught the frantic motion of Jack coming in through the back door.

As Claire was momentarily stunned, she slashed out with her knife blindly. It sliced right across the top of Rachel's wrist, drawing blood instantly. Dimly, Rachel was aware of Jack coming to her aide; he'd gone to the victim's side first, as was protocol. Apparently, Claire Allen also sensed him coming. She turned in his direction and that was the opening Rachel needed. Using the butt of her Glock for extra weight, Rachel delivered a quick punch to the side of Claire's head.

Claire blinked rapidly a few times and then tottered over. The knife clattered to the floor in the spilled paint water. She tried getting to her feet, but Rachel got to her knees, placing one squarely in the center of Claire's back. She noticed that her right arm was bleeding. She also realized that if the cut had been on the other side of her arm—on the underside of the wrist—she might be in some serious trouble.

Yeah, some manic voice inside of her head said. *You might bleed out and die before the tumor you won't tell anyone about has a proper chance to kill you...*

Jack swept in and placed a set of handcuffs on Claire Allen as Rachel pulled her arms back. "I've got her," Rachel said as she got to her feet. She did so slowly, worried that the white streaks might come back—that she'd pass out in front of Jack again. "Make sure the victim is okay."

"I'm okay," Cassie McNeil said weakly from against the wall.

"I think she might be," Jack said, pulling out his phone. "There's a cut along her side...not to deep. And what looks almost like a papercut low on her neck. But she's bleeding pretty bad from the side."

With Claire Allen in cuffs and face down on the floor, Rachel took a moment to observe her own wound. It had sliced deep enough to where it might need stitches and the bleeding wasn't as bad as she'd first feared. As Jack called in for an ambulance, Rachel took several paper towels from the roll on the kitchen counter and wrapped them around her cut.

As Rachel walked over to the wounded woman—Cassie McNeil, she safely assumed—Rachel took note of the painting on the table. An ocean scene, with a storm on the horizon. Without warning, a snippet from the nightmare she'd had two nights ago flashed through her head. Her mother, sitting on the boat she'd died in, looing lovingly at Rachel.

"It's about time you met me out on the boat," her mother had said.

This recollection was broken by the first protests from Claire Allen. "I'm not the guilty one," she said, her voice somewhere between wailing and crying. "She's a thief! She wants what isn't hers! I'm innocent! I should have my chance, too."

After that, Claire Allen started to weep. Her loud, piercing cries seemed to cover everything in the world until they were drowned out several minutes later by approaching ambulance sirens.

CHAPTER THIRTY

One of the medics from the pair of ambulances that arrived looked over the cut on Rachel's arm. After cleaning it and giving it a brief inspection, he smiled at her and started to open up a small pouch of sanitizing cream. "Well, you're not going to need stitches, which is good." He lathered the cream over the cut and then wrapped a sticky gauze around it. "I'd rest the arm for a few days, though. It's a spot that can stretch easy and it'll start bleeding in the blink of an eye."

"What about Cassie McNeil?" Rachel asked, sitting on the back bumper of the ambulance. "How's her cut?"

"Not too bad. She *will* need stitches but from what we can tell, nothing important was damaged on the inside. We're rolling her out soon, and her husband has already been notified and is on the way to the hospital as we speak."

Rachel looked over to their car. She watched as Jack closed the door after having escorted Claire Allen into the back seat. She had indeed confirmed that was her name, but they hadn't gotten anything else out of her yet.

"Thanks for this," Rachel said, showing the medic his handiwork. She hopped down from the back of the ambulance and walked over to where Jack was making his way across the street towards her.

"No stitches necessary," Rachel said. "But you should probably drive."

"Good," he said with a sarcastic smile. He then cocked his head in the direction of the back seat where Claire Allen wept softly, looking out to them as if she had no real idea why she was even there. "Now let's go get some answers."

***

Rachel found a few bags of chamomile tea in the precinct break room. Even though she was usually not a fan of tea, she needed *something* to calm her nerves. She had what she assumed was some sort of adrenaline headache, her body's response to the tension, nerves, and excitement of the last two hours or so. At least she *hoped* it was just from the adrenaline. She had no idea what she'd do if the tumor caused

141

another episode while she and Jack were right in the middle of interrogating Claire Allen. Not that there was going to be much of an interrogation. This was all just for the sake of formality; she'd pretty much admitted to everything during the tense stand-off they'd had in the McNeils' kitchen.

"I hate these interrogations," Jack said as they met in the hallway.

"What...the ones where we basically gloat about our victory?" Rachel asked.

"Sort of, but no. It's more like 'hey, we know it was you but let's see how many bullshit ways you can think of to try to worm your way out of it.' It's always feels like a waste of time."

"Then I'll take the lead on it," Rachel said, reaching for the door.

Before she could open it, Jack stopped her. "What happened back there? I saw it through the window. You were about to pass out or faint or something. So what's going on?"

"I have no idea what that was about," she said. "Maybe not enough sleep. Maybe not—"

"You're lying. I say that with as much friendliness as I can, but it's true. I don't know what you're not telling me, but if it's going to affect your work and our partnership, I think I have a right to know."

Her heart broke a bit at hearing this, but she kept the lie straight and on the surface. "I'm fine," she said.

"So fine that you thought it was a smart idea to go visit Alex Lynch?"

There was more than just a bit of bite to the comment, but Rachel let it go. She opened the door to the interrogation room and Rachel stepped inside. After a moment's hesitation, Jack joined her.

When they stepped inside, they saw that another officer had already been in to give Claire water, a pack of cheese crackers, and a box of tissues. Her eyes were red from crying and she looked exhausted. She studied both agents with equal scrutiny and when she was done, seemed not to care.

"Ms. Allen," Rachel said, "I'm going to ask you what may sound like a stupid question, but I need to make sure. Do you know why you're here?"

"Yes."

"Good. I'd like to hear it from you, though."

"I had broken into that woman's house. Cassie McNeil. And I was going to kill her. But you came in and stopped me."

"Sounds accurate," Rachel said. "And this wasn't the first time, was it?"

Claire shook her head slowly and her face seemed to go through several different emotions all at once. One moment it seemed she might start crying again, and the next it seemed like she might start screaming and cursing at them.

"We were told by a supervisor at Regency Fertility Clinic that there was recently a disturbance with you coming in to ask about your donated eggs. Is that true?"

"Yes," Claire snapped. And with that response, it seemed that her mind and her face had finally decided on a single emotion: anger. "Yes...I personally have never had any interest in having children. I work with them and that's enough for me. Most of them are quite pleasant, I guess...but some are fucking nightmares. And yes, the bad apples are enough to spoil the whole bunch for me. But at the same time, I know there are women out there that *want* to have kids but can't. So I figured I could help in that regard. I decided to donate my eggs. Honestly, the financial gain was the biggest reason but..."

She sneered here, as if she might be a little upset with herself. "For some reason, I started thinking of women using *my* eggs...a part of *my* body...it made me mad *and* it made me wonder. It made me think...maybe I would want kids at some point."

She started shaking her head here and there was a certain way her eyes trailed back and forth, the way little smiles started to form at the corners of her mouth and then disappeared, that made Rachel wonder if there was some sort of legitimate mental break that had occurred. Not too long ago, she'd read a case study about how sometimes people that donated things like kidneys would start to feel almost incomplete and even regret their decision to donate. It made her wonder if that was exactly what happened here, only on a much grander scale.

"Oh, but it just wasn't happening for me," Claire went on. "I reconnected with a man I almost married and tried to get pregnant. When it didn't work, I ended things with him and tried someone else. I even went out of the state to see if I could be artificially inseminated and *that* didn't work."

She slammed her hand down hard on the table as she spoke these last three words. Then she looked to Rachel and Jack with a stubborn, defiant look in her eye. It was almost as if she was daring them to ask her more questions.

"You used a Facebook group, didn't you?" Rachel asked.

Surprise flickered in Claire's eyes at that and then a dulled sort of acceptance. "I did. And it worked. All these stupid women just broadcasting what they had planned. Asking for prayer and positive thoughts."

Claire had not yet asked for a lawyer and the more she spoke, the easier it seemed to come to her. She had either accepted her fate and did not care or had no real idea of the severity of her crimes.

"Ms. Allen," Rachel said. "You know what this means, right? Now that you're here and have told us all of this. You know what—"

"It means I was sloppy in the way I planned, I supposed," she said. "And that I'll go jail." She snickered at this in a maniacal way, as if the world itself was unfair and she was the victim—just like she'd said back in Cassie McNeil's kitchen. "Even though I was the one having things stolen, I'm the villain here."

"With all due respect," Jack said from beside Rachel, "I think the three murders and an attempted fourth sort of make you the villain as well."

Claire furrowed her brow and scowled at them. "I'm done talking," she said. "I'd like to see my lawyer now."

"Of course," Rachel said, getting to her feet and rather glad to be leaving the room. But she already knew that based on everything Claire had just said, there were very few lawyers that would be able to get her off. She assumed the knife that was currently in evidence would also serve as a huge nail in her coffin.

She and Jack left the interrogation room, and Rachel realized she hadn't even touched her tea yet. She finally sipped from it, grimaced, and wished it were coffee. But that was the absolute last thing she needed at the moment.

"How's the arm feeling?" Jack asked. It was a genuine question—his way of politely sweeping their tense exchange before entering the interrogation room under the rug.

She looked at the bandage, amazed that she'd somehow nearly forgotten about it. "It's fine," she said. She was not as quick as Jack to get over heated words, but she was already starting to understand that his little jabs had been out of nothing more than concern.

"I don't know what got into you over the last day or so," Jack said. "But you did great. I'm trying to figure out how to write my report without making you sound like some sort of supernatural Supergirl."

She smiled, instantly thinking of her tumor. After all, didn't most superheroes have a fundamental flaw or weakness they kept hidden?

If that was indeed the case, she figured she could try wearing a cape until the tumor took her out.

CHAPTER THIRTY ONE

Because it was not too long of a drive, Rachel and Jack decided to drive home that night after the paperwork was done. The final thing they heard before they left was a bit from the forensics team. Not only was the car parked across the street from the McNeil house registered to Claire Allen, but there were several bloody fingerprints on the kitchen walls, as well as Cassie McNeil's clothes—all ID'ed as belonging to Claire Allen.

In other words, they without a doubt had their killer. Case closed.

Rachel was looking out of the window as a soft drizzle of rain started to fall. She was not tired, not exactly, but the pattering of rain seemed to try to convince her otherwise. She found herself once again thinking of her mother—more precisely, of how she died. It was strange because it was not something she'd thought of in quite some time. She supposed it was because her mother had died at an early age, leaving a young daughter behind. And she was on the edge of that very same situation.

"Can I ask you something?" Jack asked.

"Sure," she said, still looking out into the thin sheet of rain.

"Fertility and eggs and women desperate to have children…as a woman, was it hard to make it through all of this? Was that why you seemed to be a little off?"

It was a good question, and not one she had really given much thought to just yet. She'd been so distracted with her own issues and secrets that she'd somehow side-stepped the heavier elements of the case. Even stranger than that was that the biggest takeaway from the case had come from her visit to another killer, Alex Lynch.

"I think it might hit me in a few days," she said. It wasn't entirely true, but she also didn't want to seem like a heartless robot. "Right now, I'm still processing."

"Are you ready to tell me about what's been up with you lately?"

She didn't answer him right away. It was tempting, and she was so tired and distracted that it really wouldn't be all that hard to get it out. But she couldn't. Not yet. If she was going to tell anyone, Peter needed to know first.

"For now, I'm okay," she answered.

"I don't understand that answer."

She finally turned away from the darkness and the rain, setting her eyes on her partner. "If it makes you feel any better, I don't either."

***

She arrived home at 2:25. She showered, careful to avoid the bandage on her arm and slipped into bed. Peter rested a hand on her side and she backed up closer to him. She felt the words right on the tip of her tongue, the secret about the tumor, about how she only had a year or so to live. She turned towards him, doing what she could to summon the courage.

"Case closed?" he asked with the edge of a smile in his voice. It was a question he usually asked when she'd been away for a few days and they greeted one another for the first time.

"Yeah," she said, near tears.

And then, before she was fully aware of what she was doing, she was kissing him. It was tender and slow, and a few tears escaped. But Peter didn't sense the tears, only the emotion. And when she urged it on further, he did not object. They made love, slow and intentional, that was over in a quick moment of passion. Even when he noticed the bandage on her arm and tried to ask her about it, she silenced him with kisses. It wasn't the sex that Rachel needed, but the intimacy of it—to feel close to him.

When it was over, any chance that she might tell him about the tumor was gone. Somehow, it was the exact opposite of that now. Now, she figured they needed to have a discussion about why not having another child would be the best thing right now. It turned out that Jack's assumption had been right: the case had made a daunting situation with the tumor even more dauting for things at home. Currently, the idea of even *trying* to have another child made her mind and heart feel heavy.

They both fell asleep peacefully side by side and Rachel did not wake up until the sun crept in through the bedroom blinds.

She could just barely hear Paige's voice coming up from downstairs. Paige sounded as cheerful and as bright as she usually did and it made Rachel want to get out of bed and downstairs as quickly as possible. She slid out of bed and went to the bathroom where she redressed the bandages on her arm. She brushed her teeth and dressed quickly, wanting to make sure she was able to see Paige and Peter together before he stepped out to go to work.

Paige shrieked when she saw her mother enter the kitchen. She got up from the barstool where she was eating at the counter and ran to Rachel, giving her one of her intense hugs. When she saw the bandage on her mother's arm, she jumped back a bit, her eyes wide with alarm.

"Are you okay?" she asked, gasping.

"Yes, sweetie, I'm fine."

Looking into Paige's face, she started to imagine how she might tell her family about her diagnosis. It wouldn't be so hard with Peter, but how in the hell did you explain to a six year old that there was a tumor in mommy's head that was very likely going to kill her?

"Do I really have to go to school today?" she asked. "I want to stay here with you!"

"Oh, she's already tried that on me," Peter said. "No ma'am. Come on. We need to leave in about five minutes."

"I promise," Rachel said, "you and I will spend some time together this evening and do something special, okay?"

"Okay," Paige said, hugging her again.

She walked the to the door as Peter ushered her out. They shared a kiss as Paige bounded down the porch stairs. "Don't take this wrong way," Peter said, "but you seem a little off this morning. I can't quite put my finger on it. Do you need to talk through the case tonight?"

"Maybe," she said.

He eyed her with loving care for a moment and then nodded. "Take it easy today, okay? Don't overdo it."

"I won't," she said.

She closed the door as Peter headed out and then stood there for a moment, her head resting against the door. A flood of emotion came pouring out and before she knew what was happening, she hit her knees on the floor and cried until it was all out.

***

The special thing Paige elected to do that night was going over the calendar they'd made at school in order to learn the days of the week and the months of the year. Rachel and Paige sat together after dinner huddled at the kitchen table and filling it with events that were coming up through the rest of the year—the birthdays of family members and friends, holidays, trips they had planned (including the Disney trip) and special school events. It was odd to plan out her final year, but she did her best to put as much cheer and enthusiasm into it as she could.

147

She spent every moment she could with Paige, knowing that her daughter was often very clingy when she returned from trips that took her outside of the city. She stood in the bathroom as Paige brushed her teeth, said her prayers with her by the side of her bed, and tucked her in. They then read a chapter of a *Puppy Pals* book together before Rachel exited the room, turning the light out.

When she got downstairs, Peter was sitting in the living room, watching ESPN. As the day's basketballs scores and stories were discussed, he muted it and looked to her with a smile. "You know how much that little girl adores you, right?"

"It's a pretty great feeling," she admitted.

"So…the case. Your arm. Is everything okay?"

"Yes, I think so. But Peter…there's something I want to talk about before I get into the case." *Tell him, you coward,* she thought. *Peter, I went to the doctor after an episode on the training course and the doctors found something…*

"What is it?"

"I can't stand to be away from Paige for so long. Even just three days…I mean I know it affects her and it hurts me, too. Given that, I just don't know if a second child is the right choice. There are some days where I absolutely think we're supposed to have another kid, but these last four days or so…I just don't know."

It was apparent that he didn't agree, but he kept the disappointment off his face as well as he could. "Meanwhile, I think I want another one worse than I thought. I enjoy all the attempts at making one, don't get me wrong, but it's more than that."

"Peter…our jobs don't really make it easy to even maintain *one* kid."

"I know. But we could make it work, don't you think?"

"I'm not sure. Right now, at this moment, I'd have to say no."

He smiled, reached over and took her hand. "How about I lay off…give you a few more months to think it over? Maybe we can re-evaluate in like four or five months?"

"Yeah," she said, though in that moment, she knew very well that her mind would not change. Of course, by the time the opportunity for the another-kid talk came up, he'd know her secret and that would obviously take the topic off of the table.

"Can I ask why you're so on board with the idea of a second kid?" Rachel asked.

He turned the TV off completely, making sure all of his attention went to her. "The other night when I had to be late…just knowing we had to have a sitter here with Paige sort of messed with me. Sure, I know it's nothing unusual for parents to have to leave their kids with a sitter, but it just…well, it *sucked*, you know? I wanted to be here with her. It was such a simple feeling, but it made me realize how much I love that kid. That feeling has just been sort of sitting with me since then and…yeah, I think I would like to have another one to love."

Oh, you selfish jerk, Rachel scolded herself. *The longer you don't tell him about the tumor, the longer he's going to have this hope. You have to tell him…*

But even as she thought about it, Peter was leaning in and kissing her. Their bodies still seemed to be tuned up from the unexpected romp the night before. It started to get heated right about the same time Rachel felt the need to tell him about the tumor. The thought arrived almost as quickly as the surprising desire to have him again.

"Hold on," she said.

Peter smiled and looked towards the hall. "It's okay. Paige is asleep."

She smiled back and kissed the corner of his mouth. "No. It's not that. There's something I need to tell you."

He apparently saw the seriousness in her gaze because he didn't object further. He slid back a few feet to give her some space. "What is it?" he asked. "Don't take this the wrong way, but you just got all serious on me. Was it the case?"

She shook her head, trying to choose the right words. Should she just blurt it out and have it done or should she ease him into it, starting with the run out at the obstacle course? "No, it wasn't the case…though that was pretty awful. No, this happened before I got the call for the case. This—"

When her cellphone rang, she flinched. It scared her *way* too much. But as much as it scared her, it also provided an immense sense of relief. *Saved by the bell,* she thought dryly. Even then, though, she almost chose not to answer it. She had no idea when she might have the courage to get this out into the open again. She was so close to telling him—to getting this massive weight off of her shoulders.

But the FBI training kicked in hard and she had to at least check the caller display. When she took the phone out of her pocket and checked the display, she saw a name she hadn't seen on her phone in a while.

"That's weird," she said.

"What?" Peter asked, clearly a little irritated form having their kiss broken.

"It's Grandma Tate."

It even seemed odd to Peter—as it should. Grandma Tate was Rachel's grandmother on her mother's side. She lived in Aiken, South Carolina and over the last few years they'd only seen one another on either Thanksgiving or Christmas. She'd never felt close as far as Rachel was concerned, but whenever they *did* get together, there was an undeniable connection between them. When Rachel's mother had passed away, it had been Grandma Tate that had stepped in as best as she could to help Rachel's father raise her.

"It's a little early to start planning for Thanksgiving, isn't it?" Peter asked.

Rachel though so, too. And that's why she couldn't help but feel a bit nervous when she finally answered the phone on the fourth ring. "Hello?"

"Rachel! Hello, dear. How are you?"

"Hey there, Grandma," she said. She hated how southern she sounded when she said it. The rural Virginia of her childhood tended to creep out on certain words, and "grandma" was among the worst offenders.

"It's always so nice to hear your voice," Grandma Tate said. "And I know it's a bit late...too late to talk to precious little Paige, I assume?"

"Yes, I'm sorry. She's already down for bed."

"Ah, yeah, I figured. And how are you? How's work and all?"

"I'm doing pretty good," she said. Again, she was amazed with how easy the lie came. It was almost as if she was starting to convince herself that she'd never even gone to the doctor—that there wasn't a life-ending tumor residing in her head. "Same old, same old. You know how it goes."

She also hated that every conversation she ever had with Grandma Tate on the phone usually boiled down to generic one-liners and non-detailed answers. "How about you?" Rachel asked. "It's not often you make a phone call."

There was a sigh in Grandma Tate's voice when she said, "Yeah, yeah, I know. I actually called to speak to you, as you might have already figured out. I hate to be so vague, but I'd really like to meet with you in person, if possible. I can come there, or we can meet in the middle. Whatever you'd like."

"Is everything okay?"

"I believe so, yes. But there are some things I need to discuss with you and it's not the sort of thing I want to talk about on the phone."

Rachel felt a stirring of worry rise up on her...worry that was replaced by a strange sort of annoyance. "Well, that's just a little

150

cryptic," Rachel said. "But, sure...I suppose we can make that happen. When were you thinking?"

"You let me know, sweetie. I can tell you that the next week or so is not good for me. But I know how busy your job keeps you, so I wanted to make sure I allowed enough time."

"So let's shoot for the week after that," Rachel said. "I'll take a few days off and come down to visit you."

"Are you sure?"

The vague nature of Grandma Tate's news made her uneasy and no, she was *not* sure, but she felt it was something she needed to do. "Yeah, I'll make a tiny vacation out of it." She hesitated here, almost afraid to ask the question that rose to her tongue. "Should it just be me?"

There was a hint if sadness in her grandmother's voice when she answered and that was all it took for Rachel to feel quite certain that something was wrong. "Oh, as much as I would love to smother Paige with hugs and kisses, I really do think it should just be the two of us. Is that okay?"

"That's perfectly fine. Let me take a look at my schedule tomorrow and I'll call you back with a few days to choose from by the end of this week. That sound good?"

"Sounds great. Thanks so much, Rachel."

"You've got me worried, Grandma. Is everything okay?"

"Yes, everything is fine."

But Rachel doubted that. In fact, she heard something very familiar in those four words. And she could recognize it easily, because she'd been telling the same lie for the last several days.

She said her goodbyes and ended the call, looking blankly at the phone for a moment.

"Everything okay?" Peter asked, his tone indicating that he had also picked up on something fishy from the conversation.

"I don't know. She wants me to come visit her because she says there's something she wants to talk about, face-to-face."

"That...well, that doesn't sound good," Peter said.

"I was thinking the same thing."

Rachel stood up and went into the kitchen. She poured herself a glass of white wine and as she took the first sip, she saw Paige's calendar on the bar. So many little squares, some filled in with her small handwriting. Each square was a day, piling on to the backs of others, forever and ever.

Not yours, though, she thought. *How many of those boxes do you think you have left?*

She looked to the latest box Paige had filled in, a birthday party a friend had invited her to this weekend. Rachel ran her hands over her daughter's handwriting and began to weep. And when the faintest of little white flashes seemed to fill her head for the space of two seconds and then disappear, it took everything within her not to throw her glass of wine across the kitchen and fall to the floor in an inconsolable heap.

She sipped from her wine and thought of something Alex Lynch had told her when she'd visited him.

"What's it like? Being that close to...to death?" she'd asked him.

"Intimate, but in a very polarizing way. For me, it's being right there on the edge of it...knowing that one day I, too, will be on that edge, looking out the other way."

She wondered what that view would be like? Some fabled Heaven with golden streets? A tunnel of light to take her to some other life beyond the veil of this one? Or maybe just darkness, thick and never-ending...a long, unyielding sleep.

She thought of Alex Lynch as she held her wine, thinking of her Grandma Tate and her own little calendar boxes of days, checked off one square at time.

EPILOGUE

Four days later, on an overcast Monday, Rachel told Peter she was heading to work like any other Monday morning. What she did not tell him was that she'd already emailed Director Anderson and asked for the morning off. Anderson had, in turn, given her the entire day, suggesting she could use a few days after the way the case had closed in Baltimore. While the cut on her arm was healing nicely, it was still requiring bandages and was itching like crazy.

Rather than driving to work (and piling on another lie she'd been telling Peter as of late), Rachel drove to Arlington. When she parked in the visitor lot of Arlington County Jail, she felt as if no time at all had passed since the last time she was here—a visit that had also been covered with a lie to Jack.

She did not allow herself time to simply sit there and stare at the building, asking herself why the hell she was back here. Instead, she got out right away. She checked in with the same person she'd checked in with before and was escorted to the eleventh floor by a beefy-looking guard who looked to have maybe had a little too much fun over the weekend and had not yet recovered.

This time, she arrived in the small meeting room first. As she sat there and waited for a guard to deliver Alex Lynch to the room, she found her thoughts turning back to Grandma Tate. Rachel did not try to fool herself; she missed the woman terribly sometimes and it pained her heart when she realized that there was much about her childhood spent with Grandma Tate that she couldn't remember. To think she might be in some sort of trouble was scary and with every day that passed, the more Rachel did not want to make that trip down to South Carolina. Aside from her own parents, she'd not dealt with death a great deal. She'd heard how FBI agents and other law enforcement agents sometimes started to get desensitized to death if they dealt in violent cases. She found that hard to believe as she thought about potentially losing Grandma Tate.

Stop it, she told herself. *You don't even know for certain that's why she wants you to visit.*

She was rather happy when the door opened, breaking apart those thoughts. If she focused on the Grandma Tate situation for too long, she'd convince herself that the worst possible scenario was correct and she'd obsess over it. So to her strange surprise, she was nearly relieved when the same beefy-looking guard escorted Alex Lynch into the room. The guard then looked to Rachel and said, "I'm right outside."

He looked to Alex and said nothing, though his eyes seemed to say: *Just give me a reason...*

When the guard left them alone, Alex looked at Rachel intensely through his bifocals. He smiled and said, "Is your case closed now?"

"It is," she said.

"And was our conversation of some help?"

She nodded, not wanting to inflate his ego but also figuring her mere presence here was showing her hand. "Yes, it helped. I'm still trying to process exactly *how* it helped, but it did."

"So then why are you here? If it's more of just wanting to get a peek inside my head to see how a killer ticks, I'm afraid I'm really not interested in that."

"There's a cold case I've been working off and on for the last two years," she lied. "Three people killed in West Virginia in 1991. Brutal and just—"

"Do you have children, Agent Gift?" Alex interrupted.

A hundred different defenses raised up as she thought of Paige while in the presence of this man. "What business of it is yours?"

"I'll assume that's a *yes*. I ask because if I told you that I had this bratty, ill-mannered little asshole of a child that I simply could not get a handle on, would it be safe for me to assume you knew exactly what I was talking about because *you* have a child?"

"No, because my child is not a bratty, ill-mannered little asshole."

"I figured not. She has a mother that is very dedicated to her job from what I can tell. I imagine your child is maybe a bit stubborn, though naïve. Maybe always seeking your approval. Maybe your child—"

"I did not come here to discuss my child with you," Rachel growled.

Alex waved her comment away, clearly not caring. "All I'm saying is that you can't paint a single picture of every child. The kid that eats crayons or bullies others is likely not a fair comparison to your own child. The same is true of people that have committed horrendous crimes. I have done some truly deplorable things...but I believe I am still maybe not quite as bad as, say, a Gacy or a Dahmer. Do I understand the things that broke *in me* that made *me* want to kill? Yes. But trying to use me as a template for whatever other monsters you're trying to pick apart is not going to work. And quite frankly, it's fucking insulting."

It wasn't nearly the reaction she'd been looking for and his gradual defensiveness was a surprise. She'd made the mistake of thinking he'd want to talk to her—that picking his brain for thoughts and motives on a cold case might make him feel important.

"I'm not going to be your inside man," Alex said with a leering smile. "I'm not going to be your Cliffs Notes on how killers work, how we see death, how we—"

He stopped here and cocked his head, observing her like a curious animal might. There was something different in not only in his attitude, but his eyes It was as if a switch had been flicked and he was undergoing some sort of Jekyll and Hyde routine.

"What?" she snapped. The feeling that he was somehow studying her was unnerving.

"I thought I saw it when you were here last. Something...something *in* you. Something in your eyes. Remember? Something broken."

She rolled her eyes, embarrassed that she'd made this foolish choice. She started to get to her feet, not at all interested in being Alex Lynch's mental plaything.

"You're dying."

Alex spoke the words simply, but it had the effect of someone pulling a gun and shooting at her. She wheeled back around to him, expecting him to be smiling. Instead, there was an uncertain expression on his face. He nodded and added: "Aren't you?"

She knew that she did not need to actually answer—that her silence was all the answer he needed. She also felt that her face had gone about ten shades of red.

"How?" he asked. "What is it?"

"Tumor. In my brain. Inoperable."

She had no idea why she told him. Worse than that, she had no real idea why it felt almost freeing to say it.

"Let me guess. You're keeping it a secret?"

"How," she started to say, but it was suddenly very hard to breathe. "How do you know?"

"It's in your eyes...in your posture. It was in your face when I said it. You were embarrassed...which makes me think no one else knows." He finally smiled at her and when he did, his eyes looked like the hungry eyes of a snake as he looked at her through those thick glasses of his. "So now there's just one question."

"What?" she said. There was almost no volume to the word.

"What can you do for me to make sure I don't tell anyone?"

HER LAST CHANCE
(A Rachel Gift FBI Suspense Thriller —Book 2)

"A MASTERPIECE OF THRILLER AND MYSTERY. Blake Pierce did a magnificent job developing characters with a psychological side so well described that we feel inside their minds, follow their fears and cheer for their success. Full of twists, this book will keep you awake until the turn of the last page."
--Books and Movie Reviews, Roberto Mattos (re Once Gone)

CITY OF FEAR (An Ava Gold Mystery—Book 2) is a new novel in a long-anticipated new series by #1 bestseller and USA Today bestselling author Blake Pierce, whose bestseller Once Gone (a free download) has received over 1,000 five star reviews.

In the rough streets of 1920s New York City, 34 year-old Ava Gold, a widower and single mom, claws her way up to become the first female homicide detective in her NYPD precinct. She is as tough as they come, and willing to hold her own in a man's world.

When a 16-year-old girl from a wealthy Fifth Avenue family is found strangled, murdered on the eve of her society coming-out party, Ava, 1920s New York City's best female homicide detective, is called in to find the killer. She quickly learns that psychosis is pervasive even amongst the glamour of high society's wealthiest families.

Determined to find justice for the girl—and to stop the psychotic killer from killing again—Ava pries into the dangerous rings of powerful high society, finding herself threatened as she is singled out by a tycoon. Fighting for her job, trying to stop a killer, and finding herself in an unexpected romantic relationship, Ava finds herself in the battle of her life.

A heart-pounding suspense thriller filled with shocking twists, the authentic and atmospheric AVA GOLD MYSTERY SERIES is a riveting page-turner, endearing us to a strong and brilliant character that will capture your heart and keep you reading late into the night.

Book #3 in the series—CITY OF BONES—is now also available.

Blake Pierce

Blake Pierce is the USA Today bestselling author of the RILEY PAGE mystery series, which includes seventeen books. Blake Pierce is also the author of the MACKENZIE WHITE mystery series, comprising fourteen books; of the AVERY BLACK mystery series, comprising six books; of the KERI LOCKE mystery series, comprising five books; of the MAKING OF RILEY PAIGE mystery series, comprising six books; of the KATE WISE mystery series, comprising seven books; of the CHLOE FINE psychological suspense mystery, comprising six books; of the JESSIE HUNT psychological suspense thriller series, comprising nineteen books; of the AU PAIR psychological suspense thriller series, comprising three books; of the ZOE PRIME mystery series, comprising six books; of the ADELE SHARP mystery series, comprising thirteen books; of the EUROPEAN VOYAGE cozy mystery series, comprising six books (and counting); of the new LAURA FROST FBI suspense thriller, comprising five books (and counting); of the new ELLA DARK FBI suspense thriller, comprising six books (and counting); of the A YEAR IN EUROPE cozy mystery series, comprising nine books (and counting); of the AVA GOLD mystery series, comprising three books (and counting); and of the RACHEL GIFT mystery series, comprising three books (and counting).

An avid reader and lifelong fan of the mystery and thriller genres, Blake loves to hear from you, so please feel free to visit www.blakepierceauthor.com to learn more and stay in touch.

DEATH (AND APPLE STRUDEL) (Book #2)
CRIME (AND LAGER) (Book #3)
MISFORTUNE (AND GOUDA) (Book #4)
CALAMITY (AND A DANISH) (Book #5)
MAYHEM (AND HERRING) (Book #6)

ADELE SHARP MYSTERY SERIES
LEFT TO DIE (Book #1)
LEFT TO RUN (Book #2)
LEFT TO HIDE (Book #3)
LEFT TO KILL (Book #4)
LEFT TO MURDER (Book #5)
LEFT TO ENVY (Book #6)
LEFT TO LAPSE (Book #7)
LEFT TO VANISH (Book #8)
LEFT TO HUNT (Book #9)
LEFT TO FEAR (Book #10)
LEFT TO PREY (Book #11)
LEFT TO LURE (Book #12)
LEFT TO CRAVE (Book #13)

THE AU PAIR SERIES
ALMOST GONE (Book#1)
ALMOST LOST (Book #2)
ALMOST DEAD (Book #3)

ZOE PRIME MYSTERY SERIES
FACE OF DEATH (Book#1)
FACE OF MURDER (Book #2)
FACE OF FEAR (Book #3)
FACE OF MADNESS (Book #4)
FACE OF FURY (Book #5)
FACE OF DARKNESS (Book #6)

A JESSIE HUNT PSYCHOLOGICAL SUSPENSE SERIES
THE PERFECT WIFE (Book #1)
THE PERFECT BLOCK (Book #2)
THE PERFECT HOUSE (Book #3)
THE PERFECT SMILE (Book #4)
THE PERFECT LIE (Book #5)

THE PERFECT LOOK (Book #6)
THE PERFECT AFFAIR (Book #7)
THE PERFECT ALIBI (Book #8)
THE PERFECT NEIGHBOR (Book #9)
THE PERFECT DISGUISE (Book #10)
THE PERFECT SECRET (Book #11)
THE PERFECT FAÇADE (Book #12)
THE PERFECT IMPRESSION (Book #13)
THE PERFECT DECEIT (Book #14)
THE PERFECT MISTRESS (Book #15)
THE PERFECT IMAGE (Book #16)
THE PERFECT VEIL (Book #17)
THE PERFECT INDISCRETION (Book #18)
THE PERFECT RUMOR (Book #19)

CHLOE FINE PSYCHOLOGICAL SUSPENSE SERIES
NEXT DOOR (Book #1)
A NEIGHBOR'S LIE (Book #2)
CUL DE SAC (Book #3)
SILENT NEIGHBOR (Book #4)
HOMECOMING (Book #5)
TINTED WINDOWS (Book #6)

KATE WISE MYSTERY SERIES
IF SHE KNEW (Book #1)
IF SHE SAW (Book #2)
IF SHE RAN (Book #3)
IF SHE HID (Book #4)
IF SHE FLED (Book #5)
IF SHE FEARED (Book #6)
IF SHE HEARD (Book #7)

THE MAKING OF RILEY PAIGE SERIES
WATCHING (Book #1)
WAITING (Book #2)
LURING (Book #3)
TAKING (Book #4)
STALKING (Book #5)
KILLING (Book #6)

CAUSE TO SAVE (Book #5)
CAUSE TO DREAD (Book #6)

KERI LOCKE MYSTERY SERIES
A TRACE OF DEATH (Book #1)
A TRACE OF MURDER (Book #2)
A TRACE OF VICE (Book #3)
A TRACE OF CRIME (Book #4)
A TRACE OF HOPE (Book #5)

Made in the USA
Monee, IL
16 January 2022